MW00929862

I Am

I Am

A Novel

Brian K. McGee

iUniverse, Inc.

New York Lincoln Shanghai

I Am

Copyright © 2007 by Writers Guild Association

All rights reserved. No part of this book may be used or reproduced by any means, graphic, electronic, or mechanical, including photocopying, recording, taping or by any information storage retrieval system without the written permission of the publisher except in the case of brief quotations embodied in critical articles and reviews.

iUniverse books may be ordered through booksellers or by contacting:

iUniverse
2021 Pine Lake Road, Suite 100
Lincoln, NE 68512
www.iuniverse.com
1-800-Authors (1-800-288-4677)

This is a work of fiction. All of the characters, names, incidents, organizations, and dialogue in this novel are either the products of the author's imagination or are used fictitiously.

ISBN: 978-0-595-44957-6 (pbk)
ISBN: 978-0-595-89276-1 (ebk)

Printed in the United States of America

CHAPTER 1

▼

(A fall setting at a college campus. Students of all types, either in groups or walking alone are seen through the area. Gothic kids, skaters, preps, jocks and thugs are shown. Moving to the inside of a fairly large classroom. Students scramble looking for seats. The bell rings. The professor walks inside the classroom)

Narrarator: It's hard being yourself at times when you're living in a world that doesn't want you too. So many people that are different, but normally think the exact same things. That's where I come in. I am what I like to be known as recycled goods. I have a history of problems and issues that most people go through today while others try to sweep them under the rug. I was a suicidal kid once and sometimes I still am, but that just makes it easier for me to be more of a dick to people. No, I don't carry an arsenal ready to commit mass murder just so I can get arrested or killed and say it was because no one liked me. That's just stupid. No, I learned a better way to get people's attention and feel better about myself in the process. It's called being myself. I'm the dark-skinned one with the glasses.

Professor: All right guys. Settle down. Find your seats and find them quick. (The class settles down) Let us begin. To start, I would like to congratulate you all on a job well done on your reports on dating in modern society. Kudos to all of you. (He turns to his desk and takes an organized stack of papers and passes them out to the front rows of desks) A big job well done to the two of the classes best and yet, most competitive students. (A teenage girl is shown sitting at her desk. She plays with her cinnamon colored hair as she writes at her desk. Miss. Becky Sloan and (Next a teenage black student is shown. He writes at his desk. Some of his friends sit around him talking and trying to get him in the conversation, but the student remains focused on writing. He quickly stops as one of the students taps him with a set of papers) Mr. Deshawn Keith. Congratulations to the both of you. Now, continuing our discussion. Can true love exist in modern day society? That is the topic of the week. Who here believes that? Hands? (Scattered students throughout the classroom raise their hands) Don't be shy. Anyone else? (He sees Becky not paying attention as she talks to her friends) Miss Sloan? (She quickly looks to him as the teacher says her name) Care to share your point of view?

Becky: Well, sure. (Deshawn shifts his head a few inches in her direction. He then scoffs lightly and turns back to his book) I think that in our generation, true love really does exist. I believe that anywhere a man and woman can meet and click almost instantly. Be it at a coffee shop or a friendly meet at a chat room. It doesn't matter. (Deshawn scoffs again) I for one am in a very loving relationship. (Deshawn snickers) The man that is in my life now is a very trustworthy and caring person. (Deshawn whispers in his friends' ear and they both laugh under their breaths. Becky looks to him at the corner of her eye and looks back to the teacher) As I was saying, true love is a powerful thing. The youth of today may have changed, but the values we expect in finding a relationship are still the same. Yes, today women expect a little more support from the male, but what would you expect?

Deshawn: (He sighs) Not much from chicks like you. (Deshawn and his friends snicker again. She looks to him)

Becky: I'm sorry, but what the hell is so funny over there?

Deshawn: Your mastery of silver tongue amazes me. How long did it take you to perfect it?

Becky: The truest of the losers speaks. Is that jealousy I hear?

Deshawn: (He turns to her as he is sniffing at the same time) What is that stench? Smells like used rubbers. Have you been doing dirt before class again?

Becky: And how would you know what that smells like? Last time I checked, the only ones you see are still on the shelf at the grocery store. (Her friends laugh)

Deshawn: (Chuckles) That's funny. You know I saw something else there that reminded me of you as well.

Becky: And that would be?

Deshawn: A chicken on a rotisserie. (His friends laugh wildly)

Becky: (Sarcastically) Ha ha. Very funny.

Professor: (He smiles and looks at the rest of the class) Hey now. Even though my next remark is going against the policies and regulations of this educational institution, as your professor I have to say this. I am beginning to find an interest in this tension. Communication is key to understanding the differences of things. Now Deshawn, I want you to take the feelings that you have now and use that. Tell us why do you object to what she says?

Deshawn: Sir, I object to her even being conceived. Getting back on topic, it's because there's no such thing. True love doesn't exist in our modern society. If that were the case than all of us would be happy. No one would suffer because they would know that someone besides that person's family cares for them. There would be no teenage suicides and post-adolescent depression. No one would carry on the burden of having to cry about how they never had anyone in their life and how mommy and daddy never loved them. If that pain never was to be felt then the parents' marriages would be happy. Then the kids would be happy. Once the kids are happy, then they meet other opposite kids who are also happy, get together, get married and continue the cycle.

Professor: So then will true love ever exist?

Deshawn: Tough question to answer. Only a portion of the general population can answer that. The remaining people have been brainwashed with focusing only on the physical aspect of who they meet, then worrying about who that person is on the inside later. By the time that person does that, they've already been cheated on and are working on starting over. It's the small group of those that really do care for one another that actually express the true meaning of that word.

Professor: And just how have people been brainwashed?

Deshawn: Through media meaning, magazines, television and movies. Think about it, all of them express the fact that in order to feel happier with themselves they need to be with a person who would make other brainwashed people accept them more. Imagine yourself in the Olympics and a top model is the gold medal. If you won, how would your "audience" feel?

Professor: Pretty happy I guess.

Deshawn: Right. Now imagine if you won the bronze which was a normal girl who is a very sweet person, but not as good looking. Then how would they feel?

Professor: I suppose a little awkward.

Deshawn: Exactly. So with that point what does that make you think?

Professor: That by dating someone that the person knows that their acquaintances would accept, those type of people are the only ones sought after.

Deshawn: Exactly. Yes, a guy wants the hot chick and yes, the girl wants the super stud. The point is that once time finally starts to go by, will you really feel happy with the person you met for everyone else, or are you going to be happy with the person you met for yourself?

Professor: So it doesn't exist?

Deshawn: Hell, no! Society now has taken a really messed up thought processing shift. It's like nowadays, in order to get a second look, you have to pass the proper qualifications first. Almost like you're applying for a job. You either have to have the right amount of this or the right amount of that in order to be properly processed. Which is stupid because by doing that, you completely throw out the whole concept of having the word chivalry in our vocabulary in the first place.

Professor: What about the nice guys? Do the nice guys get processed as well?

Deshawn: (He chuckles as he responds sarcastically) Well, yeah. Think about it. Complaints are spewed out almost everyday on how all a woman wants is a nice, sweet, and caring person in their life. Then the moment they find one, they either put them in the friend pile or toss them like bad trash. Just so the women can run off with a dude that pretends to be nice just to give up another pair of drawers to add to the dude's collection. Then when the woman gets cheated on, they're back to square one. All boarding the same complain train. A woman wants a nice guy, she meets one. Finds out he's genuine, then puts him in the friend pile. Just so they can go after the popular, but yet mysterious guy. The nice guy goes out of his way to make the girl feel special. What does she do? (Mimicking) Why, thank you, you're so nice. Now run along back to the pile. I've got some real guys to date. (In his normal voice) Then when something happens in their relationship, the nice guy is only supposed to be the shoulder to cry on, lean on, but never to be used to hold on. We are designed only to listen, never to be heard. To be seen, but never to be touched. To bear the heart that gives us life, but never be allowed to share it? We are the masters of pro bono B.S. female psychology. (The students roar in applause)

Professor: So what about the saying on how nice guys finish last?

Deshawn: What about it?

Professor: You think that's a lie as well?

Deshawn: (He responds sarcastically) Yes, I do. Nice guys can never finish last. We can't finish a race we no longer qualify for. Once we hear the gunshot, Bam we wind up pulling a muscle and have to quit. The true women worth running for are always missing in action. (At that moment a female student walks in the classroom. She readjusts her book bag and looks around for a seat. She hears Deshawn speaking and notices an empty seat behind him. She takes another look for a closer spot and walks to the empty desk to sit down)

Professor: So then, what do they want?

Deshawn: Neither side knows. Men and women are like a rubix cube from hell. Neither side knows what they want. For women, it's like asking someone with multiple personality disorder. They give you one emotion one minute, and then once you want to further the relationship with them, their whole story changes to tell you something different. For men, it's like the same thing. Everything's cool once he and someone else go out, but he quickly loses interest in the female and goes to someone else. Then the only question to ask is, why would you like someone in the first place if you don't like talking to them once you start dating. Since the more sincere and caring guy doesn't fit the right qualifications physically, they're cast aside so that the other party can search for someone who does? That in itself has proven to be the dumbest thing to have happen to anyone. Yes you look good and are hot as hell, but you're as stupid and useless as suburban gangster rapper. Yeah it's nice visually, but it still doesn't mean it makes sense.

Professor: Any reasonable solutions?

Deshawn: For both sides to quit being so stupid and think realistically. Stick to the real truth and not your own perception of it.

Becky: Boring.

Deshawn: Case in point. If society keeps living the way it is now, then we're forced to live the life of prostitution like certain people behind me. You know, living only to give it up to any good looking person that walks by.

Becky: Maybe if you get out of that smurf cave you call a room every once and a while. It just might be possible that you could find someone hanging around to talk to. Just be sure that you're wearing your big boy shoes first. We women don't like having to feel like we're talking to some lost grade school children.

Deshawn: You know, I would tell you to choke on something, but mine don't reach that far. (Class reacts shockingly)

Becky: Please, like yours can even reach at all. (Class reacts again in the back round) Why don't you take your elf looking self back to the forest you came from ok?

Deshawn: Nice one. Better to fly away as an elf than use your method which is spread eagle. (Class reaction intensifies. The new girl stares at Deshawn as she tries to cover her laughter. She looks around to make sure no one watches) Being able to hold multiple passengers and have the frequent flier miles too? I swear, if I didn't know any better, I would mistake you for being a seven forty seven airline jet. Is it true that you were awarded the MVP at the abortion clinic? (Becky is unresponsive and the class is shocked) Yeah, I thought so. As I was saying, our society has turned itself into some kind of popularity contest. This is not "The Bachelor "or "American Idol". This is the reality of building a real relationship with someone.

Professor: Good point. Very nice, I like that. You see, that's why I like hearing you speak. You're never afraid to say the opposite of what people think. I admire that and I want you to keep focus on that gift you have, all right?

Deshawn: (He salutes him) Yes sir. I'll do my best.

Professor: Your best is all we ask for. Keep up the good work, all of you.

CHAPTER 2

▼

Deshawn Narrarates: My upbringing has got to be the most awkward part of my life. My family consisted of four people. Just like every modern day family, it was my mother and father, my sister and me. Here's where the fun part kicks in. My mother is a total head case. No, I mean literally she's a head case. She was diagnosed with disorders that even I can't pronounce. My sister was just flat out stupid. She's got major issues too, but combine that with an 80's generation rebel attitude and that spells get the hell away from me. My father is the only one in the family who's actually stable. The only one to hold what was left of the family and teach me how to live was him. Mainly because he knew that since I'm his only son, he can't risk losing me too.

(After class, Deshawn walks out a set of double doors with his backpack over his right shoulder. Becky walks out as well a few moments later. The professor rushes out after Deshawn)

Professor: Mr. Keith!

Deshawn: (He stops and turns around) Professor Peters. What's up?

Professor Peters: (He hands him a staples set of papers) You left without this. (Deshawn takes it and looks at it for a moment and looks back to his professor)

Deshawn: You made a mad dash from the bottom of an auditorium to out here, just to give me an "A" paper?

Professor Peters: An "A" paper that's well deserved.

Deshawn: But this isn't the only thing you wanted to bring to my attention right?

Professor Peters: I was talking to the dean last week about a position I had posted for an assistant. He handed me a possible list, but I had to turn them all down.

Deshawn: What for?

Professor Peters: Cause I just handed my main candidate his "A" paper.

Deshawn: (Shocked) What?

Professor Peters: Congratulations Mr. Keith. With what you're learning now, plus having a bit of teaching under your belt, you should do just fine in the future.

Deshawn: Why did you pick me though?

Professor Peters: After what you just pulled in class today, why shouldn't I have picked you? Mr. Keith, you have a gift. How you perceive things, expands the common mediocre lifestyle everyone else is used to. With that state of mind you have the ability to break down walls that are meant to be broken. Who else has the courage to say that simple-minded people are just that, simple?

Deshawn: I thought it was just meant to piss people off?

Professor Peters: That too of course. (Deshawn chuckles. At that moment, the new girl who sat behind Deshawn walks out of the entrance doors and looks to a sheet of paper) Deshawn, we need more people like you. Let me ask you something, what do you think about narcissism?

Deshawn: Blame the parents.

Professor Peters: Hypocrisy and ignorance?

Deshawn: Against my beliefs.

Professor Peters: Living in a fantasy world?

Deshawn: What do you think being a teen is all about?

Professor Peters: (He pats him on the arm) Now do you understand?

Deshawn: (He chuckles) All right, I got it. I'll take the job. Now, I gotta make tracks. See you tomorrow sir.

Professor Peters: Bright and early.

Deshawn: Good afternoon sir. (He turns and walks away. The girl reading the paper spots Deshawn, but is too late to get his attention. She slowly follows him. Deshawn makes his way to a round bench and sits down. His friends welcome him to join in on the conversation. All are excited as the conversation continues to go on. The new girl stands against a nearby tree watching the group. She doesn't notice Becky and her friends standing a few feet behind her talking. Becky later notices the new girl and looks at her as the girl begins to walk to Deshawn)

Deshawn: I don't know what the big deal is anyway. I just said my piece that's all.

Jose: (He exhales the smoke from his cigarette) Once you learn the basics of eating you could give the whole pie.

Deshawn: Shut up fool.

Quinn: He's got a point. You're too nice. When you gonna stop being such a pussy dude?

Deshawn: You say that like it's a bad thing.

Jose: Well it is. People take advantage of that and it sucks. I know you know that from the past couple girls you been with.

Deshawn: So what. It isn't like I've got a complex or nothing. The chicks that dumped me just lost someone special. I see no fault in that.

Quinn: Yeah you did. You lost someone who wears the same size clothes you non-eating bastard.

Deshawn: Hush up peasant!

Erika: He's not being serious.

Quinn: Yeah I am. Erika, look at him. The boy's so skinny, he can use an ankle sock for a belt and still have room to spare.

Erika: Shut up Quinn. D, you really are a great guy. You never cheat and you're always reliable. It's just sometimes people see that as a weakness and take advantage of that. You've got to be mean sometimes. Jose, tell him.

Jose: That's right. Next time a girl does you dirty, tell her to kiss your ass until twelve-thirty. Then, just open your hand and proceed to give the girl five across the eyes as hard as you can. Then you start choking the hell out of them and start yelling. Don't you ever do me like that again in your life! Well, at least that's what I tell chickens who get flip with me.

Deshawn: (His eyes get wide and he uses them to look around for a moment. He then turns to the girl) Ok. So, anyway Erika how are you? (Deshawn looks back to Jose) My bad man. (Jose gets him in a headlock for a moment and lets him go) You guys do have a point though. I just can't do the whole unfaithful thing.

Quinn: You have to. We are programmed to cheat. Not everybody's perfect. So stop trying to be. You can't go into a buffet and have the same food everyday. Disperse yourself. By doing that can you truly find your place in life. So pick up a plate and get a taste of everything you can.

Deshawn: Quinn, just what the hell are you talking about?

Quinn: I lost my train of thought. I had an idea going and I lost my place. Next topic please.

Jose: I got an idea.

Deshawn: What?

Jose: Graduation.

Deshawn: That's six months away. Save it for later.

Jose: No, no, no. I got to say it now, otherwise I'll forget. Check this out. We rent a limo.

Deshawn: That's so eighties.

Jose: No, no. A stretch Escalade limo armed with spinners and hydraulics.

Deshawn: That is by far the dumbest thing I have ever heard in life. You can't put hydraulics on a limo.

Jose: That's why it's going to be built like an RTD bus. You know with that splitter thing in the middle so it turns better. Hook it up with some hydraulics, huh? Rolling with the gangsta lean and having the bass thumping in the back. I mean we can turn that sucka into the ultimate alpha and omega pimp mobile. Dig this, neon lights on the side that read, "The Boom-Boom Room".

Deshawn: The boom-boom room? God, you need to get out more, but wait, now I've got an idea. How about we get a taxi with the same thing? It's a little bit more realistic, but we'll still get the same end result.

Jose: What's that?

Deshawn: We'll still look stupid as hell.

Jose: (He punches him in the arm) Nerd!

Deshawn: (He punches him back) Douche bag!

Erika: Hey! Quit it before I slap the piss out of the both of you!

Jose: Damn girl, why you always wanna beat people up?

Erika: Cause it's what I'm good at stooge.

(Jose and Deshawn exchange more punches at each other and Erika slaps the two of them around. The girl walks up from behind Deshawn)

Stacey: Hi. Sorry for interrupting. You're Deshawn right?

Deshawn: (The group stops. Deshawn turns to look at her. Erika looks to her from the corner of her eye) Depends on who wants to know.

Stacey: (She holds out her hand) Hi. I'm Stacey. I'm new to the school and I sit behind you in class.

Deshawn: Well, hello there Stacey. Nice to meet you. Yes, I am Deshawn, but my friends call me D. (They shake hands for a moment and let go. He then points to his friends) That's Quinn, Jose and Erika. (She waves to the group and smiles. Erika just lifts her head to her)

Stacey: Hi. (They wave back) I heard you in class today. I was pretty amazed.

Deshawn: Why thank you. Please. Take a seat.

Stacey: Thank you. (She takes her bag off her shoulder and sets it on the ground and sits down next to him) May I ask you a question?

Deshawn: May I give you an answer?

Stacey: (She laughs) Sorry. I was kind of shocked at what you said in class today. I'm not saying that like it's a bad thing. It's just that I've never heard anyone say the things that you said before. You're not always that angry are you?

Quinn: Only when he steps on the scale.

Deshawn: (He looks to him) Shut up. (He looks back to Stacey) No, I'm not. I'm just different. No big thing.

Stacey: So just what are you?

Deshawn: A lot of things actually. I'm a mix of every group. I don't like being just one particular person. Call me multi talented.

Stacey: So, what person is that?

Deshawn: The leader of course. Follow the road opposite from the fools.

Stacey: Interesting words. One more question. I needed to meet someone here to help me find my way around this place. Can you help me do that?

Deshawn: Who did you have in mind?

Stacey: Well, hopefully you can help me, if you're free?

Deshawn: (In confusion) Me? Ok then well, yeah, sure. I can do that.

Stacey: (She gets up and grabs her bag. She puts is back over her shoulder and continues to look at Deshawn. She smiles) Great. Is tomorrow good?

Deshawn: Yeah. That's fine.

Stacey: Good. I'll see you around then.

Deshawn: All right.

Stacey: Bye. (She walks away)

Erika: (Mimicking) I'll see you around then. Tramp.

Deshawn: Come on. Cut her some slack. She's new here.

Jose: Maybe, but (He looks behind Deshawn) oh damn!

Deshawn: What?

Jose: Becky and her backup groupies.

Deshawn: (In confusion) What? (He turns to see her walking towards him. Her friends go in another direction towards Stacey out of view from the others) Aw hell!

Becky: (She looks to the group) Hey guys. (She looks to Deshawn) Hey Deshawn.

Deshawn: Can I help you with something?

Becky: I just wanted to talk to you about some things. First of all, I really didn't appreciate what you were saying about me in class.

Deshawn: I'm flattered, thank you. That really means a lot.

Becky: I haven't made my point yet. Look, I've been thinking that maybe we should call a truce?

Deshawn: A truce? Right. What kind of game would this be?

Becky: No game. Our hatred for each other has gotten so old. I feel like growing up first instead of playing these childish games with you. (At that moment, a young man wearing a football jersey whistles to her and signals for her to come to him)

Deshawn: Well, it looks like you still got a ways to go. I see that you still haven't gotten past the prostitute stage yet. Still running at your masters' call?

Becky: It's not what you think.

Deshawn: That's because you're not getting it on out here. (He looks to his watch) At least not at this hour. You know, shouldn't you be going through the stains on your sheets to find out who you baby's daddy is or something?

Becky: You know what, forget it. I come over here trying to make peace and you do nothing, but spit it back in my face. Just forget it. (She turns to walk away, but D stops her)

Deshawn: Wait. Look, I'll make peace if you show me first. You already know that I can do it. Can you though? (The jock runs up to Becky)

Jock: Hey Becky. Let's go. (Deshawn looks at the two. The jock sees him and starts to stare him down) You got a problem or something small fry?

Deshawn: As a matter of fact I do. I got problems with lanky bastards thinking they own everything. (The jock pushes Becky to the side and Deshawn stands up staring face to face with the jock. Deshawns friends quickly get up and stand behind him)

Becky: (She looks to the jock) Matt, please.

Matt: You're lucky you little freak. Next time when your buddies aren't around you're mine.

Deshawn: And I'll be the only one standing, pole smoker.

Jose: The only way you get to him is through me. Since I don't see that happening anytime soon, what's your next move? In the other direction or in a body bag? Take your pick. So either chill out or I knock you out. Take your pick.

Matt: (He looks at the two) Let's get out of here. (Matt and Becky walk away)

Deshawn: Dick. Let's get the hell out of here. (The group walks away. Becky finally meets up with her friends with Stacey in the middle of the group)

Becky: Hi, you must be Stacey right?

Stacey: Hi.

Becky: Listen, you're new here right? Let me be your after school guide.

Stacey: (In confusion) After school guide?

Becky: Yeah. Someone who can teach you the ins and outs of getting yourself adjusted in the best possible way here.

Stacey: Sorry, but I already have someone helping me with that.

Becky: (She leans back) Really? Just who is this lucky person?

Stacey: I sit behind him in class. Deshawn Keith.

Becky: Really? Good for you. Well, since you're in our class, I should probably get you at least a little caught up on our last project. While we're at it you look like you need a few good girlfriends by your side as well. Come with me.

CHAPTER 3

▼

Deshawn Narrarates: I was a major geek to the tenth degree back in the day. The only thing missing is the coke bottle glasses I wore in grade school. I still am though. It keeps my brain moving you know. I have so many friends of all types now. Thugs, skaters, goths, punks, give or take a few preps here and there, but I don't care really. They respect me and that in itself is one of the greatest gifts you could ever give a person who never got it. Some see it as strength, others really like seeing it as a weakness. For people with that type of arrogance, always look for a reason to show it off. Not with me though. Always the small and quiet ones, right? The ones you don't want to mess with.

(Later on that day, Deshawn walks down a hallway listening to music while Matt walks down the opposite side. Matt angrily walks closer in Deshawn's direction and later bumps into him)

Matt: Watch where you're going dork!

Deshawn: (He removes the headphones from his ears) Why don't you do the same, dick!

Matt: (He walks up to him) What did you say freak show?

Deshawn: I didn't stutter. Dick.

Matt: You know, you talk a lot of mess for being so small. You're lucky I don't kick your little ass right now.

Deshawn: Well then, why don't you get rid of all that hot air in your big ass head so you'll know how to understand me better? Either that, or fix those antennas you call hair to get better reception. (Matt pushes him. Deshawn quickly tackles him to the ground and the two start fighting. Moments later, a teacher spots the two and runs towards them. Time passes and Deshawn and Matt sit in the dean's office in chairs distant from each other)

Dean: Well, isn't this shocking? I don't get it. Right here in front of me, I have the two best male students in this school. Matt, your love for playing in football and academics was just a few of the main reasons why you're here in the first place. Deshawn I'm still stuck on. Do you know just how many of your teachers practically fought to have you enrolled in this school? Not to mention Professor Peters personally choosing you as his assistant. I just can't understand how this can happen?

Deshawn: That one's easy. Captain Blue Balls over here decided to test his manly hood to me by trying to start a fight with me in the hallway.

Matt: I wasn't trying anything. If I was your little ass would be in the hospital right now.

Deshawn: Yeah, what dream did you get that from jerk off?

Dean: (He pounds his fist against the desk) That's enough! Both of you! Now you leave me no choice. Both of you are suspended.

Deshawn: What?! What the fuck kind of shit is this?

Dean: You watch your mouth!

Deshawn: I will not watch my mouth. I damn near get killed and I'm getting the blame?

Dean: If Matthew is causing a problem then seek assistance from either security or one of the staff on this campus.

Deshawn: How do you figure I do that? After I come out of the hospital? I'm sorry, but I prefer to defend myself when I have to, not when it's given to me as an option. He tried to harass me and I defended myself. That's it. So keep the fingers on this one. (He points to Matt and stands up) I'm out of here. (He walks out of the room and slams the door behind him. Deshawn walks into his room and throws his jacket on the floor. He turns on his stereo loud and lays on his bed and plays rock music. Jose walks inside. Once he hears the music he puts his hands over his ears and starts to stagger wildly towards the stereo. He finally turns it off and breathes deeply grabbing his chest. He looks to him) Okay. Hi.

Jose: Damn it man. How many times do I have to tell you not to listen to this crap you demented freak?

Deshawn: It's just rock man. You make it sound like I'm listening to monkeys getting it on or something.

Jose: Because that's what it sounds like.

Deshawn: (Sarcastically) Ha ha. I like my music preference. Anything that sounds good to me, I listen to.

Jose: But, you're black?

Deshawn: And you're brown. Look, listing to what I listen to doesn't change the way I am. I am unique. If I want to be a skater one day I will. If I want to dress in all black or look like a thug, the only thing you can do is deal with it. So you can kiss my half nappy afro.

Jose: (He grabs the back of Deshawn's hand) What color is this?

Deshawn: I'd like to think of it more like a caramel or a mocha color. Besides, that's almost like asking me if I like lynching. (Jose lets go of his hand and steps back as he laughs at him)

Jose: My bad man. Remind you of your older sister?

Deshawn: Please, as long as I've tried erasing her from memory, that one moment never escapes me.

Jose: Why you sound all pissed?

Deshawn: All American football ass jock tried to fight me in the hallway today.

Jose: What?! I'm gonna kick his ass. (He tries to reach for the door)

Deshawn: No need. He's probably still in the dean's office right now anyway.

Jose: You straight?

Deshawn: (Quietly) Yeah. I'm just sick of dicks like him thinking that they can just push around whomever they want and get away with it. Bastard learned real quick that you don't pull that with me.

Jose: One of the many things that I like about you. You got bigger balls than half the people in this school. You talk to your family yet?

Deshawn: Nope.

Jose: Why not?

Deshawn: Never found a reason to yet.

Jose: It's your family.

Deshawn: I know. Ever since I moved out we haven't talked.

Jose: So what are you waiting for?

Deshawn: Nothing.

Jose: You do know that the not-talking thing will keep going if neither side talks first.

Deshawn: What's that supposed to mean?

Jose: That means that in order to squash this madness, you might have to bite the bullet and start talking first. Neither side has to have a reason to do anything, but someone has to say something.

Deshawn: I might take that into consideration, but I can't do that right now. I'm going to do it though. Soon.

Jose: That's good. How much homework you got?

Deshawn: None. I already finished before school let out.

Jose: Still heavy on them books.

Deshawn: Yep. Knock them out so I don't have to deal with it later. (He says with a smile) It's what keeps me satisfied.

Jose: Yeah, you have fun with that.

Deshawn: So, what's everyone else doing?

Jose: Well, Erika's out shopping with some of her friends and Quinn is doing some work on the system in his car.

Deshawn: Right on. Want to hit up a movie?

Jose: Fine with me. Just don't go yelling at screen if the movie sucks like last time.

Deshawn: Yeah, I do remember scaring off some of the people there.

Jose: More like the whole room.

Deshawn: (He laughs) All right, I'll try this time. (He gets up from his bed and they both leave.

CHAPTER 4

▼

Deshawn Narrarates: My friends are the most important thing I have in my life right now. It's crazy how we all met. Quinn and I met at a party he was hosting and he spotted me dancing. Jose was when he was about to beat up some generic thugs and I decided to step in and lend a hand. Erika was special. I was being beat up at school one day and thrown in a locker. Next thing I know she comes around at the last second and beats the hell out of all of them and helped me out. We all looked out for each other from when we all met until now. They play a big role in keeping my feet on the ground. They're why I'm still around now.

(Next day in class, Deshawn sits in his desk talking to his friends.)

Quinn: Hey, before I forget, Kevin's holding a party tonight at his spot. You're going right?

Deshawn: Sounds like an idea.

Quinn: Well you need to man. We need that "Shakedown" special you two always bring.

Deshawn: I don't know. I think I'm getting a little rusty. I don't know if I have the right motivation to go to this thing.

Jose: How about this, if you don't go I'll break your legs?

Deshawn: (He thinks for a moment) Then I wouldn't have to go to class or to the party. So you'll be doing me a favor.

Jose: All right then. How about this? If you don't go, I'll tell your pops that you gave up on that little project of yours.

Deshawn: All right hold it. That's the only pressure technique that will get me to do anything. I'm not stopping on that. Just let me know when I should be getting ready. (Stacey sits down behind him)

Stacey: Hey, D!

Deshawn: Hey, Stacey!

Stacey: How are you doing today?

Deshawn: Good and you.

Stacey: Just fine. Were we still going to hang out after school?

Deshawn: Yeah. Just meet me after class.

Stacey: All right. I have another question. Just what is the deal between you and Becky anyway?

Deshawn: Too long of a useless story. (Stacey looks back to see Becky sitting with her friends. Becky doesn't see her. She looks to the teacher as he walks in the classroom)

Professor: Good morning class. How is everyone? Today is going to be a fun day for you all. Your mid-term project (The class moans in disappointment) will be about you. (Students yell in the back round)

Student #1: Booo!

Student #2: Get off the stage!

Professor: This project will cover what makes you who you are. What defines you? Why do you do the things you do? I want you to start from the earliest you can remember and from there. Include the music you listen to. What movies you like watching. What you read and so on and so forth. Deshawn and Becky, I'm expecting my usual A pluses from the both of you all right. I don't want you doing this on your own. I want you to get with everyone you know and get the feedback you need. This will help give your minds more power to keep going. I want you all to give me everything you have on this all right? I know you can do this. You guys and gals ready? All right then, let's get started.

Deshawn: What the hell? "What defines you?" Screw that, I'm not writing jack. (Jose hits him in the head with a pencil) Damn it!

Jose: Just for that, you're writing five.

Deshawn: Why? I don't have much to talk about?

Jose: Fool, I've known you for years on end. Trust me, five pages you can do while sleeping.

Professor Peters: Becky. What type of person do you think you are?

Becky: Well, I thing of myself as a woman who knows what she wants in life and also knows how to get it.

Deshawn: STD's don't count. (The class is in awe)

Becky: Oh really? So just what do you think you are besides a loser?

Deshawn: Not a walking sperm bank like yourself. What I am is me. That's as far as it goes. Do I need anything to define me? No I do not. I am being myself, while you are trying to fit into something you don't need to fit into.

Becky: So let's bring the question to you. I mean, since have this amazingly large perception on things. Where do you fit in at? Either you're too white for the blacks or too black for the white people. There's a word for people like that and it's called an Uncle Tom. (The class is shocked. Erika starts to get angry, while Stacey looks in shock)

Erika: If that skank doesn't take that back, I'm gonna kill her.

Stacey: Now hold on. That is very offensive. So what do you expect him to do act and dress like he came out of a rap video in order to be accepted someplace? Or would you prefer him at act like he has multiple personality disorder whenever people from different groups come around? (Deshawn looks confused as she keeps going) The only thing that he along with everyone else can be is themselves. Isn't that right Deshawn?

Deshawn: (He pauses for a moment) Yeah. Right on the nose. (Erika leans next to him)

Erika: What the hell just happened?

Deshawn: It sounds like she's defending me. That's a first.

Becky: Look, people like him have no place. He's not an independent person, he's just there and hanging around people like some kind of leech.

Deshawn: And what does that make of you and your knock-off pussycat dolls? Please, the only thing that you're good at being is the tourist attraction between your legs. (The class goes wild) You expect me to act like your perception of this? (He points to the back of his hand) So, I guess that means I have to either rob a seven-eleven, play basketball, or make a suck-ass rap album in order to be noticed as people to someone as stupid as you. Am I close to being right on how you see things? Check and mate.

(Another kid sitting beside Deshawn leans up to him and pats him on the back)

Student: 'Sup y'all.

Deshawn: What up Kev.

Kevin: Not much, here. Just making sure you're cool. (He pulls out a piece of paper and hands it to Deshawn)

Deshawn: The hell is this?

Kevin: What's going down at the party?

Deshawn: Why don't you just tell us?

Kevin: I don't want people who are not invited to hear. (Deshawn is speechless as he looks in confusion. Kevin later slaps him in the back of the head)

Deshawn: Ow! What the hell was that for?

Kevin: Because (He slaps him again) you think to damn much. That's what gets you stupid in the first place.

Jose: (In thought) You know what, you're right. (He slaps Deshawn)

Deshawn: Would you stop! Please? I get it. I'll read it now and see you at the spot.

Kevin: Cool. (He leans back)

Erika: Oh, before I forget. (She pulls out a manila folder and hands it to Deshawn) Special delivery.

Deshawn: Right on. Thank you for getting this for me.

Erika: Anytime. (She looks to Stacey then back to Deshawn) Wait until after class. (Stacey leans to Deshawn)

Stacey: What's with the secrecy?

Deshawn: Family project.

Stacey: Plan on sharing anytime soon?

Deshawn: Sorry. This is one of those things that you have to know me really well to be a part of it.

Stacey: I see. (After class, Deshawn and Stacey walk around the campus talking) All right, spill it. What is the deal?

Deshawn: With what?

Stacey: With you and Becky. Why do the two of you hate each other so much?

Deshawn: I told you already. It's very long and yet very boring story that you don't want to hear. It was one of those moments in time that you wish that you never wanted remembered. Plus, I don't want to waste any time with it.

Stacey: You're not wasting it when the other person doesn't mind listening. Besides, school's over right? So, we have the rest of the day to get to know each other. (Deshawn looks to her for a moment and looks away. He looks back to her)

Deshawn: All right. Back in middle school when I was working on my master's for revolutionizing loser lifestyle and geek ethics. Becky gets into this thing with one of her boyfriends and in a desperate act of recovery. She decides to search to find a lotto ticket.

Stacey: Lotto ticket?

Deshawn: Quick pick.

Stacey: Oh.

Deshawn: She writes a note to me in class talking about hooking up. Now remember, I was a geek during this time, so my success in dating was like comparing a professional hooker to finding Jesus. So, me thinking that my luck has finally changed, I decide to give it a shot. The school day hasn't even ended yet, and already I've got people looking at me and laughing. Come to find out that she only used me in order to make him jealous. So, there I was, even more depressed. I became the laughing stock of the school yet again.

Stacey: So what did you do?

Deshawn: Nothing, until fate finally kicked me in the ass. I was going to the bathroom when I heard some pretty funky things going on in there. It was the happiest day of my life when I heard her name being called.

Stacey: Oh, my god.

Deshawn: I know.

Stacey: I don't understand. How was that the happiest day of your life?

Deshawn: Because before I went, one of my friends was talking about taking her out that night. He was one of the popular people at the school. Once I told him, the only thing he could do was tell everyone he knew which led to the whole school knowing about it. She was branded ever since.

Stacey: Did that help you at all?

Deshawn: A little. I made some new friends which grew faster than I thought it would. Once high school started, that was the moment that I dubbed her and her group of remaining friends the "Freshman Slut Brigade".

Stacey: That is amazing. I never would've imagined.

Deshawn: Neither did I. Who would've thought that a loser from Aurora, Colorado could become one of the most popular kids in school.

Stacey: I don't know. If I knew you then, I probably would have. (Deshawn does not respond) What? Frightened that a girl has interest in you?

Deshawn: No, it's just that … (Before he finishes his sentence Quinn runs to him)

Quinn: 'Sup D. We've been looking for you. You remember the plan tonight right?

Deshawn: Of course I do.

Quinn: So let's roll. We got stuff to do before we go.

Deshawn: Cool. Wait, hold up. (He takes out a pen and a scrap of paper from his bag. He begins writing on it. A few moments later he hands the paper to Stacey) Here.

Stacey: What's this?

Deshawn: My number. There's a party going on tonight and I want you to go. (She looks confused) I know it sounds like moving to fast, but what better way to talk and get to know each other than at a party.

Stacey: Won't it be loud there?

Deshawn: You'll see what I mean.

Stacey: All right.

Deshawn: (He walks away) Phone's always on. Anytime all right?

Stacey: (Laughs) All right. (Deshawn and Quinn walk off. Erika sees the two running towards her. She looks behind them to see that Becky is walking up to Stacey and the two walk away. She looks back to Deshawn)

Erika: What the hell took you so long?

Deshawn: My bad. Sorry. So what you got?

Erika: A lot of shopping in only a few hours. Talking to your new friend?

Deshawn: A little chit-chat. Nothing else.

Erika: Whatever works for ya.

CHAPTER 5

▼

Deshawn Narrarates: I can't remember the last time a woman actually had an interest in me. Probably because no one except my friends did. Every relationship I've ever been in was crap. Either they started out smart and then became stupid, or just wanted to stomp all over me as much as they could. That's why to them I'm a stone. Emotionless and cold at times. I can't risk breaking again.

(Away from being seen, Becky talks to Stacey)

Becky: So how did it go?

Stacey: Very well. He's really a great guy. I still can't see why you hate each other so much?

Becky: Long story. (She quickly stops herself) Wait a minute, he told you what happened?

Stacey: Yeah.

Becky: That little troll. I think we should reorganize our little study sessions.

Stacey: What do you mean?

Becky: I think you should hang out with me a little more. You'll get adjusted more quickly.

Stacey: But Deshawn is doing a good job on his own.

Becky: Trust me on this. The boy has problems.

Stacey: Are you just saying all these things because of what he did?

Becky: Get your story straight. If it wasn't for me, he would still be a low class hack with no friends. After hearing what happened, at least do me the honor of giving me the benefit of the doubt. I helped him when no one would. So I did it in cruel way, but hey, that's the way life is for some people.

Stacey: Ok. So what happens now?

Becky: Keep talking to him. Get him to open up to you and then let him know that I want to make peace with him finally.

Stacey: Why can't you tell him? (Becky looks to her in disbelief) Oh, right. I forgot. Sorry. (Later on in Deshawn's room, he and his friends are sitting around. Deshawn stands in front of the window as they watch him open up the manila folder)

Erika: Well?

Deshawn: Sorry, but my x-ray vision is on the fritz right now. I actually have to take these papers out to look at them. (He reads for a little and stops. He shakes his head in disappointment and throws the papers in the air. His friends become disappointed as well) I can't believe this crap.

Jose: All these years and still nothing. How long has it been? Four years?

Deshawn: Five years, seven months, and sixteen days.

Erika: We could call or petition. Do something to make them tell us.

Deshawn: No dice. They'll only give me some B.S. excuse why I still can't get the information I need.

Quinn: You're not giving up are you?

Deshawn: I can't. I've come too far to quit now. I just hope she's okay.

Erika: (She gets up and walks to Deshawn) She has to be. She is. Don't worry, as long as you don't give up, neither will we. Right guys?

Jose: No doubt.

Quinn: True until the end man.

Deshawn: Thanks guys. The bad news is not that I know that she's okay, but what if I'm too late and she's not.

Erika: She'll be fine. Stop worrying about it okay? You promise? (Deshawn doesn't answer) D! Promise me. (A moment passes. He then nods his head in acknowledgement)

Deshawn: Yeah.

Erika: Great. Now, what are you going to wear to this party?

Deshawn: Still playing mother I see?

Erika: Nope. Just playing the role of being the only female you know that you only look at, but are too scared to touch. (Jose and Quinn react in shock)

Deshawn: Wrong. I am only scared of what happens after I do touch you.

Quinn: Damn!

Erika: And what's that? You're gonna use the "L" word?

Deshawn: Ha! Not on your life girlie. You know that word is no longer in my vocabulary.

Erika: Then what?

Deshawn: That you would. (Jose and Quinn react more wildly)

Quinn: Big D! You going to be working on the plumbing? I see she's due for an appointment. Check this out I got the tools at the crib, just say when.

Deshawn: Indeed, but not now. We got a party to get ready for. So let's get moving. I need all the energy I can muster for tonight's shakedown.

Erika: What about what's her face?

Deshawn: Stacey? I do not know. I gave her my number, but I doubt that she'll use it. (At that moment his phone rings. He pulls his phone from out of his pocket and answers it) Hello? (He looks in confusion) Wicked. I was just talking about you. So what's up? Really? Yeah, just meet me in front of my dorm around six or so. Cool? All right, later. (Stacey hangs up her phone and looks at it. She sets it down.)

Stacey: Tonight at six. (Stacey is in Becky's room. She leans against her dresser next to her window while Stacey lies on her bed)

Becky: I should get you ready for this party.

Stacey: This isn't some scam is it?

Becky: What do you mean?

Stacey: From what I understand, the two of you hate each other. Once you saw me talking to him, you began referring everything about him as an experiment of some kind. D's a nice guy and I think I'm starting to like him.

Becky: How good for you. I simply ask for you to assist in helping me in this one little favor and you're starting to back out now?

Stacey: It's not like that. I would love to hang out with you and your friends.

Becky: But what?

Stacey: But, I would really like to get to know D on my own terms. Not someone else's.

Becky: Fine. We can work with that. If you feel happy around him at one time and with us at another, then that's fine with me. Come here. You need something to wear to this party. (She opens her closet. Stacey gets off the bed and walks to the closet as Becky begins to take a few clothes from the rack and looks at them. Later on in the day, Stacey stands outside of Deshawn's dorm on a bench. She looks around for a moment and checks her watch. At that moment Deshawn speaks from behind her)

Deshawn: You could've waited inside where it's warm. (Stacey turns around to see him with a flower in his hand and a slight grin)

Stacey: I thought you said wait outside your dorm?

Deshawn: Yeah, but inside the lobby. You know strange things do happen when the sun goes down around here.

Stacey: (She giggles and looks at his flower) Is that your way of apologizing for almost becoming a creature of the night?

Deshawn: This? No. I just like trying to be nice sometimes. It's not everyday that people see me like this. I actually bought a real one. You can tell by the smell.

Stacey: (She smells the flower while keeping her eyes on Deshawn) I like it. Seriously, is this how you treat all of your dates?

Deshawn: Date? (He begins to stutter a little) No, not really. Usually my dates consist of club hopping with friends and mild underage drinking. Sorry, I'm just a little nervous.

Stacey: Don't be. You're doing fine so far. You're really sweet.

Deshawn: Thanks. It's just using the word "date" got me kinda edgy. I mean it's not everyday that … (He stops) Here. (She takes the flower from him and holds it close to her. She looks into Deshawn's eyes and they share a small moment. He looks away for a second and looks back to her) We should go.

Stacey: Yeah. (She stands up. Deshawn notices that it is a little cold and Stacey's jacket might not be enough to keep her warm. He takes off his coat)

Deshawn: Here.

Stacey: (She sees him holding his coat for her) Why thank you. What about you?

Deshawn: As long as you're fine, which you are, I'll be okay. (She laughs for a second)

Stacey: Thank you. (She adjusts her hair and looks around) So, which way D?

Deshawn: Well there's the short way which is driving. Then there's the long way which is walking down that way. (He points behind her to a dimly lighted path. She turns and looks. Deshawn reaches in his pocket as he looks at how dark the path is) Yeah, bad idea. Come on, I'm parked out front. (She quickly grabs his arm)

Stacey: I don't mind walking.

Deshawn: You sure?

Stacey: If I didn't want to do it, I wouldn't have asked.

Deshawn: True. All right, you win. Walking instead of riding it is. Shall we?

Stacey: Lead the way.

(They begin walking down the path)

Deshawn: So, while we got time. What about you? What's your story?

Stacey: Well, I moved here from Atlanta.

Deshawn: Really?

Stacey: Yep. Down south.

Deshawn: And you wanted to move here? I take it you don't worry about snow much?

Stacey: No. Not really. It's real warm there, so it's kind of hard getting adjusted to the cold.

Deshawn: Well, you picked the wrong place to say that. The winters here normally last for about eight months give or take.

Stacey: (She stops) Are you serious?

Deshawn: You don't watch the weather channel that much do you?

Stacey: I never had a reason to.

Deshawn: You'll learn as I did. Just be sure to stock up on goose-down coats in the next few months.

Stacey: Oh my god. (They keep walking)

Deshawn: That's what I say when I see the first few sprinkles of the snow. Normally it includes a large amount of curse words in it.

Stacey: (She laughs) Oh really. So there is a hint of badness in you after all.

Deshawn: I wouldn't go so far as to say that. I have had my fair share of awkward moments.

Stacey: Like what kind?

Deshawn: Did you ever see a person curse at a movie screen because of the movie he thought was good, really sucked?

Stacey: Are you for real?

Deshawn: Yep. I keep a record of consecutive wins in Ripley's Believe It or Not for the world's most skeptical, but yet influential man they ever knew.

Stacey: Oh really now?

Deshawn: No. I just wanted to add a little shock to the conversation. You'll get a lot of that when you hang around me.

Stacey: I'm starting to like it already. So, are you always this nice of a person?

Deshawn: Not really. Most of the time, I'm a complete dick. Part of growing up I guess.

Stacey: Then what's with the coat and the rose?

Deshawn: I have high morals. Call it chivalry. First impressions are the most important, so I went out of my way to make a good first impression.

Stacey: Which you did. I appreciate that. I will have to return the favor someday.

Deshawn: No need. You being happy and having a good time is more than enough.

Stacey: That I can't do. You see, you are a good guy and I want you to know that. I have a problem being generous too. It's just a way of saying thank you properly for me.

Deshawn: So just you being happy isn't a proper way?

Stacey: Nope. That's just something that you'll have to learn as well about me.

Deshawn: Well, I never turn down an opportunity to learn something new. If that's a challenge you're throwing at me, then I'll take it.

Stacey: Do you always take challenges this quickly?

Deshawn: Depends if it's worth it or not?

Stacey: Well is it?

Deshawn: Will I be graded?

Stacey: If I say yes?

Deshawn: Then I'm not doing it.

Stacey: Then no.

Deshawn: So this is extra credit then?

Stacey: Nope.

Deshawn: Then where's the challenge?

Stacey: If we can be more than friends when you pass.

Deshawn: (He thinks for a moment) Oh, I get it. I thought that having a girl roommate isn't allowed though?

Stacey: (She playfully slaps him on the arm and laughs) Silly.

Deshawn: I'm just joking. I'll be a good boy.

Stacey: You're doing a good job already.

Deshawn: Why thank you. I try at times.

Stacey: Do you always try like this?

Deshawn: No, usually I just break out into a really bad stuttering zone and immediately get into geek mode.

Stacey: Your stutter wasn't all that bad though.

Deshawn: You weren't around when I had it in grade school. For example; how long does it take for you to say the A, B, C's?

Stacey: Probably less than a minute, why?

Deshawn: Back then, you could watch the series of Roots, take a nap and have a snack. By the time you return, I would be close to letter F.

Stacey: Oh my God. Was it that bad?

Deshawn: Very. You ever have your own teacher purposely skip you for reading in class because of it? Once my teacher got wind of it, the whole school knew and switched me from the big bus to the little one.

Stacey: That sounds so mean.

Deshawn: That's not the worst part of it. You ever met someone who was a certified nut before?

Stacey: You sure don't show it?

Deshawn: Well, add a pinch of optimism and you can fix any problem.

Stacey: What was it?

Deshawn: The list was too long for me to pay attention to it. Plus I was real young when I got it anyway.

Stacey: What did you do to fix it? Therapy or medications?

Deshawn: Both for a while. Then that's when I noticed something. Even though talking to therapists is cool, they're not always the answer for people who felt like I did. It was the fact that that person had someone to talk to because nobody else wanted to. As far as medications were concerned it's nothing, but a poor excuse of making the situation worse instead of better. The second people see you have a problem they wanna drug you. Then the moment those same people have a form of a conflict with themselves, they take similar medications to make themselves look better. Shortly after it, leads to taking drugs that make them worse to feel happier. Once you see the stupidity from the way people act you find that much needed loophole.

Stacey: Which is what? (He looks to her as they walk. He releases a grin and gives her the finger. Stacey opens her mouth in awe and chuckles. Deshawn lowers his hand) And what is that supposed to mean?

Deshawn: The symbol that I'm my own man. Having the ability to do and say what nobody else can. The ability of having independent thought.

Stacey: So what else can you do?

Deshawn: Wouldn't you like to know.

Stacey: Actually, I would. (Deshawn becomes speechless)

Deshawn: Damn.

Stacey: What?

Deshawn: Normally, this is the part where something happens so that I don't have to get into that like in the movies. You actually caught me off guard.

Stacey: Oh my god. Are you stumped?

Deshawn: No, no. I'm not stumped. I said I was thrown off guard.

Stacey: So what's your response then?

Deshawn: How about this, think of the world as a one-way road. It's one that everyone drives on and everyone is accustomed to using. You throw a roadblock in that and that person is clueless on where to go. Keeping your mind open to new possibilities increases awareness in my opinion. To many single-minded people trying to get you to think the way they think and act the way they act is another form of slavery. Taking away from you what's important to follow what other people think is important.

Stacey: Intriguing state of mind.

Deshawn: It's been known to piss people off quite a bit.

Stacey: I kinda like it. I take it you get picked on a lot when you were a kid?

Deshawn: I never did bother with it really.

Stacey: You seem to have out done yourself with it.

Deshawn: Thanks. I catch some heat every once and a while. Not like I used to though, luckily.

Stacey: Did the other stuff ever get that bad after you stopped thinking the way you did?

Deshawn: It caught me off guard a few times, but thanks to my friends I learned to control it more.

Stacey: That's good to hear.

CHAPTER 6

Deshawn Narrarates: The party scene has always been big with me. It's gotten to the point where if one goes down, I'm always the first to know. Why, you ask? Because I am a flat out nut that knows how to party.

(Party noise is heard in the back round. Deshawn looks to the house and points to it)

Deshawn: Here we are. Party central. You ready?

Stacey: With you here, I'm ready for anything.

Deshawn: All right then. Dress right?

Stacey: Check.

Deshawn: Smell right?

Stacey: (She sniffs Deshawn's coat and her shirt) Double check.

Deshawn: (He takes a few sniffs around her) You pass with flying colors.

Stacey: All right. (They give each other a high-five)

Deshawn: Let's do this. (They walk to the house)

Stacey: How wild do these parties get?

Deshawn: Not real wild, but don't worry. You're in good hands.

Stacey: I hope so.

Deshawn: I know so. (They enter the house. The music plays loudly and people either dance around or stand talking to others. In one corner, people stand and engage in freestyle battles with each other and outside stand smoking. Deshawn and Stacey continue through the cluster of individuals. Jose spots Deshawn walking through)

Jose: Hey!

Deshawn: (He spots Jose and grabs Stacey's hand as they walk to him) What up!

Jose: You made it!

Deshawn: You think I wouldn't?

Jose: You never turn down a good party.

Deshawn: You must be smoking the wrong stuff if I do. Where's Q at?

Jose: Getting a drink. (He looks to Stacey) You're Stacey right?

Stacey: Yes, indeed.

Jose: A word of advice. You picked one hell of a guy to come to this party with. He's making sure that you're good right?

Stacey: He's doing a good job of showing me that so far.

Jose: That's cool. Just do me one favor though.

Stacey: Name it.

Jose: People like him are one in a million. Don't waste it.

Stacey: I wouldn't even dream of it.

Jose: Just making sure. (Quinn comes up from behind Jose with two cups in his hand)

Quinn: Lookie here. I knew there was a reason I got two drinks instead of one.

Deshawn: One for me?

Quinn: Yeah here. (He hands Deshawn the cup and quickly pulls it back) Oh that's right I forgot. You got a date tonight.

Deshawn: I'll take good care of her. Don't worry about that.

Quinn: Not her fool! For me. I need a designated driver. (He takes a drink from one of his cups) You're first on my list. (He looks to Jose) Do me a favor and keep an eye on Mr. Bentley for me. Don't want him leaving a brother stranded.

Deshawn: Only if you make me want to.

Quinn: Now be a good boy and hold that.

Deshawn: (Sarcastically) Thanks. (Quinn hands him a cup)

Quinn: Gotta stock up. I'll be black.

Deshawn: You keep drinking like this and you won't be for long. (Erika walks up from behind Deshawn) I swear that guy takes down more drinks than a prostitute does dicks.

Erika: Got room for one more passenger?

Deshawn: (He turns to her) Depends. You'll have to go through a screening process. That could take weeks.

Erika: Is there a quicker way?

Deshawn: A hug would do.

Erika: (She laughs) Anything for family. (She hugs him. She adjusts her hair as she steps back. She looks to Stacey) I see you brought your new friend. You are Stacey, right?

Stacey: Yes ma'am.

Erika: That's nice. (She grins and then turns to Deshawn) D, can I pull you to the side for a second?

Deshawn: (He pretends to act nervous) I'm not in trouble am I? I mean I just got here and can't function with negativity thrown at me at such an early time.

Doing this could cause a complete and total mental break down and I can't have that at this time. Unless I've had a few drinks first.

Erika: (She cuts him off by slapping him in the back of the head and laughing) Move. You're such a kid.

Deshawn: I know. Why do you have to be so hostile? (They walk outside and sit on a small set of steps leading to an alley beside the house) What's cracking?

Erika: Just checking up on you.

Deshawn: Thanks mom.

Erika: So, how is she? (She picks up her drink and takes a sip)

Deshawn: She's cool. I'm a little off track that she's coming at me this quickly though.

Erika: I noticed. If something were ever wrong, would you tell me?

Deshawn: Always, you know that.

Erika: I just don't want what happened last time.

Deshawn: It won't happen.

Erika: That's what you said the last time.

Deshawn: Well, last time I was still naïve and stupid. This time, it's different.

Erika: How?

Deshawn: I'm not opening up that side of me for a while. I already made that promise to myself years ago.

Erika: When we almost lost you right?

Deshawn: Yeah.

Erika: I remember you couldn't talk for weeks. We had to beat it out of you in order to get a syllable.

Deshawn: Yeah I know. I'm not falling for those traps anymore.

Erika: What if you do though? Will you at least tell us?

Deshawn: Of course I will.

Erika: I hope so. It's just that after watching what you did and how you became, I don't want to see that side of you again. I already enjoy seeing what you've become.

Deshawn: So do I. (Chuckles) You have no idea how much the group means to me. Trust me, I don't want any part of the old me again.

Erika: I hope so. (Inside the house Quinn talks to Kevin)

Kevin: Where's D at?

Quinn: I think he's outside talking to Erika.

Kevin: Could you get him for me. We got some things to do.

Quinn: All right hold on. (He looks and finds Jose) Yo Jose! (Jose looks to him through the crowd) We got shakedown. Get D!

Jose: Check. (He runs outside)

Erika: I want you to be careful okay?

Deshawn: Always. I'm going to make sure I don't fall for the same trick twice.

Jose: (He bursts through the back door and holds it open as he fakes being out of breath) D. It's getting crazy in there. We need your help. Hurry!

Deshawn: What the hell? (He runs inside and Erika follows. Once inside everyone applauds. Kevin stands next to the stereo in a large empty circle. Deshawn smiles)

Kevin: All right now. Everyone here knows that this can never be a good party without D here to help do one of the things that we always got to do with him around. (The people react wildly) So hurry up and get over here. (Deshawn makes his way to the Kevin. Stacey walks to Quinn)

Stacey: What's going on?

Quinn: They're about to do what's called a shakedown.

Stacey: And that is?

Quinn: Every time Kevin and D party they always do this. It's kind of like a dance competition. They've been doing it since high school.

Stacey: D dances too?

Quinn: D does a lot more than you think. After every dance battle, someone else comes in to challenge D's freestyle skills. So far the boy hasn't lost yet. Kicks ass every time. Excuse me. (He runs to the stereo and puts a cd in)

Stacey: Really. (She looks to Deshawn as he stands next to Kevin)

Kevin: All right. Every party that me and this cat are in, we have to do the shakedown. Now who's going first?

Deshawn: Do I really have a choice?

Kevin: Not really.

Deshawn: We shoot for it. (Quinn starts the music)

Kevin: All right. (Both move to the music while the crowd screams in excitement. Deshawn and Kevin lean forward and get ready to play rock, paper, scissors while moving to the beat. They start. One, two, three. Kevin wins. He steps up and begins his routine. Deshawn jumps back a few steps as the crowd gets louder. He places his hand on his chest as though he is in pain. Erika and Quinn help him out. Deshawn's pumps his chest mildly as his friends help him take off his shirt. Seconds later, Deshawn quickly throws off his shirt and begins his form of dancing utilizing his skill of pop-locking and break dancing. Stacey watches in shock as she sees him move across the floor with so much grace. The dance continues and Deshawns' final move shocks the crowd. Once he is finished both stand side by side and do a group pop and lock routine that excites the crowd even more. Another song plays and a circle is formed. Erika puts on a hat and cocks it to the side and jogs next to Deshawn. The group gets ready for a rap battle. Everyone at the party watches as they jump around and get wild. One of Deshawn's friends goes first. The one rapping starts throwing out line after line of cracks at Deshawn and Erika. Erika gets mad and Deshawn holds her back. Erika looks to Deshawn)

Erika: May I please?

Deshawn: You may. (He signals for her to go next. Erika begins rhyming and later passes to Deshawn. Deshawn steps up and gets going and almost every verse he says has everyone going wild. The group stomps to the beat and saying the chorus of the song together. Once the song is over, Stacey walks to Deshawn applauding for him)

Stacey: Amazing. Just how many more secrets do you have in that concealed hat of yours?

Deshawn: More than you think.

Stacey: Think you can show me some?

Deshawn: (He places his hand on her forehead) I sense strong energy from within you. You could make a good part-time student.

Stacey: What about full-time?

Deshawn: Moving the wheels kind of fast, aren't you?

Stacey: Call it woman's intuition. I believe that I have found something worth understanding more.

Deshawn: What's there to understand?

Stacey: Why I can't stop liking you so much.

Deshawn: Really? That's a first.

Stacey: First time for everything.

Deshawn: That is true. No denying that, but it's just that it's been a fairly long time for me. Normally I work in steps.

Stacey: Indulge me then. What steps do you normally take?

Deshawn: (Sighs) Well for starters, if this is what you're looking for, it's going to take me a while to open up actually.

Stacey: If time is really what's needed, then let's make it.

Deshawn: You're serious about this?

Stacey: I work in steps too. I also know something special when I see it. I see that in you. You're a good person. You aren't afraid of me, are you?

Deshawn: No. It's wondering if your interest is merely an act for yourself or someone else. Is it me that you want for good? Or is it me that someone else wants for bad?

Stacey: It's for … (She is cut off as Becky walks up from behind her)

Becky: Well look at what we have here. How are you doing Stacey? Deshawn?

Stacey: Becky! Hi. How are you doing?

Deshawn: Yeah Becky, who are you, I mean how are you doing?

Becky: Good Deshawn, thank you. Please tell me that you thought about our conversation on a truce?

Deshawn: A little.

Becky: And?

Deshawn: I'm still thinking. Years of fighting, forgotten in a day? It takes a little bit longer for something like that to sink in completely.

Becky: Well, the offer still stands.

Deshawn: So it shall. When I'm ready to take it, I will.

Becky: Sooner that later?

Deshawn: If it gets flakey, then a hell of a lot later that sooner.

Becky: Understood. Stacey, come talk to me for a little while.

Stacey: Okay. (She slowly walks to her)

Deshawn: Hey Stacey! (She turns to him) Don't look directly into her eyes. At least not until our curse is broken and the moon is full. (He looks at her with weird eyes and she giggles as she walks away. Kevin walks up from behind Deshawn and taps him on the arm)

Kevin: What's up man?

Deshawn: Not much here. I didn't know that Becky was going to be here.

Kevin: Party crashers. No big deal.

Deshawn: Didn't know she knew Stacey either.

Kevin: Nothing gets past her. Besides, tricks know how to get around. Just brush it off.

Deshawn: She did a good job of letting it get past me though.

Kevin: What's that supposed to mean?

Deshawn: Nothing. Do you know where the others are?

Kevin: Well Jose decided to mistake the tequila for water, Erika is still outside, and Quinn is talking to the girls wearing a tool belt and a hard hat. Where he got them from is beyond me.

Deshawn: Looks like I'll be outside then.

Kevin: If anything happens, I'll let you know.

Deshawn: Thanks.

CHAPTER 7

▼

Deshawn Narrarates: I try my best to be a good man around the new people I meet. Sometimes it works while other times it doesn't. Either way, I still wind up getting hurt somehow. This girl maybe different, but that doesn't mean I shouldn't still be skeptical about what she tells me.

(He walks outside and stands in front of Erika) Got room for one more?

Erika: Please, I've been trying to save it from all of these drunk frat boys looking for a good time.

Deshawn: How about a regular boy?

Erika: Always. Come here. (He sits down next to her) So, what's up?

Deshawn: Not much. A little confused though.

Erika: About what.

Deshawn: Well, for starters, Becky's here.

Erika: (She reaches into her pocket) I knew I brought my biking gloves for a reason.

Deshawn: Not that. Stacey started talking to me about going further until (Erika cuts him off)

Erika: Becky showed up and suddenly the two know each other.

Deshawn: Exactly.

Erika: Pays to be your closest friend.

Deshawn: I know. Everything was cool up until that moment. Now I can't seem to shake the feeling that she's up to something.

Erika: Becky?

Deshawn: Worse.

Erika: No worries, I'll take care of it. Excuse me. (She stands up. Deshawn quickly grabs her arm and stands up as well)

Deshawn: Hold it. Just what are you planning on doing?

Erika: If the two of them are planning something nasty then I'll just give them a little behavior modification. Works all the time.

Deshawn: There's not really a need for that.

Erika: When is there? When she chews you up and spits you out like everyone else did? I've seen you suffer for to long to have to watch you go through this again.

Deshawn: I understand what you're saying, I really do. I already told you, I'm not falling for the same trick twice.

Erika: The trick changed, but the setup stays the same.

Deshawn: So then what should I do, give everyone I have an interest in the brush off.

Erika: If you do, then you'll fall right back into that pit you promised me that you would never fall back into.

Deshawn: (He quickly responds) And I'm not going to Erika. I'm just asking for your help on this, that's all.

Erika: (She stops for a moment) You really want to do this?

Deshawn: Not really, but at least help me make sure that this is a real deal. No violence please.

Erika: (She holds up two fingers and sighs with a bored look on her face) Scouts honor.

Deshawn: Thank you.

Erika: I will go and talk to them. Be right back. (She attempts to walk inside, but Deshawn calls to her)

Deshawn: Erika. Did you really bring the gloves?

Erika: No silly.

Deshawn: Ah praise Jesus. You're not lying to me, are you?

Erika: Of course not. If I did I would ruin this outfit I went out of my way to wear tonight.

Deshawn: Just making sure. One more thing, be gentle with them.

Erika: I'll do my best.

Deshawn: You're not only the best. You're the greatest.

Erika: That's because I learned from the master. I'll be back in a minute. (She walks inside the house. Becky talks to Stacey)

Becky: So how's it going?

Stacey: Pretty well actually.

Becky: And Deshawn?

Stacey: I like him.

Becky: As long as you leave it at that. Irregardless, he hasn't been an ass at least one time?

Stacey: No. He has a good heart, he's sweet, smart, but a little in the shadows when it comes people liking him for more than a friend.

Becky: He must've got that from me.

Stacey: I'm starting to get a hint of that a little more.

Becky: Look in order for this work I need a little bit more information about D. Can you do that for me?

Stacey: I still don't understand what you want from him.

Becky: I want you to coerce him into this truce. You saw the way he acted when I tried to be nice to him.

Stacey: I know.

Becky: Look, the only thing that I realized that has become the most important, is to graduate knowing that this feud between me and D is squashed and never to be spoke of again. Is that to much to ask?

Stacey: I guess not.

Becky: See. You understand after all. Now here's what I want you to do. (Before she can explain Erika walks up from behind the group)

Erika: Hey Stace. (Erika looks to Becky with a smile on her face) Hey ho. (She looks back to Stacey. Stacey turns to her) Can I talk to you for a second?

Becky: What did you call me? (She tries to stand up. Erika raises her hand in front of her as she quickly responds)

Erika: Trust me bitch, pissing me off is never a good idea. So unless you want that weave snatched out along with the rest of your fake ass, I suggest that you sit back down please and thank you. (Becky sits back down with nothing to say)

Stacey: Wow. Yeah, sure. (She walks to Erika. As they walk, Becky calls to her)

Becky: We'll talk later. I'll see you at school. (Erika and Stacey walk away. One of Becky's friends leans to her)

Megan: God I hate that chick. One question; Just what are you planning anyway?

Becky: (She watches the two leave in disgust) Just like I said; (She looks to her friends) I want this feud to end. I plan on using young Stacey to get as much information as she can on the ever-so elusive D, so I can use that to finally crush that little bastard once and for all. In the end, D will be so broken that he'll finally be out of my hair and before she knows it, we'll have a new friend to sail into graduation with.

Rebecca: Don't you think that's a bit harsh. Why don't you just tell him you're sorry and end it there?

Becky: It took me to long to rebuild my reputation after what that freak show did. Don't you get it? I refuse to be beat by a low-class punk. Did he have what we all had? No, but somehow he got it. I don't appreciate that all that much. He's hated by the people who are with us, and adored by the people who are against us. Which over the years have spanked us pretty hard.

Megan: What is it about him that people love so much? I always thought he was a certified nut case since grade school.

Becky: I heard he was. You should have seen him. Always moping around like a beat up elephant and coming to school with self-inflicted scars on his arms. I always wanted to know myself what was up with him.

Rebecca: That's why you are using Stacey. To find all that out and get him back into being the damaged goods. That and increase her interest in him so I can hit him where it hurts, the bastard.

Becky: Something to that extent.

Megan: You are so evil.

Becky: Only on the inside. (Later Erika talks to Stacey outside. Both stand on opposite sides of an alleyway leaning against the houses closely built to each other. Erika holds a beer as her arms are loosely crossed)

Erika: So how's school going for you?

Stacey: Good. I'm making a lot of new friends which is cool.

Erika: That's good. I noticed that you and Becky seem to be getting pretty close.

Stacey: We talk every once and a while.

Erika: So I take it that you know about her and D then?

Stacey: Yeah, D told me everything. He doesn't worry about it much.

Erika: That's D for you. Once he sees that something is too childish to be used as an adult, he brushes it off quicker than anyone else. He's a real smart guy when it comes to serious topics. Other that that, he's a nut. (Before Stacey can respond, Erika cuts her off) The only one who can call him that are his close friends so there's no reason to question what we call him.

Stacey: I noticed, but he seems to be a little resistant when it comes to relationships. Almost as if he doesn't believe in them.

Erika: He doesn't. He's grown to despise anything and everything that has to do with that subject.

Stacey: But why?

Erika: All of his previous relationships have been hell. Dating him out of pity, breaking up with him in front of his own home, to even a girl he was dating for a few years cheated on him with someone he used to work with. So you can begin to understand a little bit as to why if you approach him like you have been doing, he always pulls back.

Stacey: I want him to like me the same way I like him though. He's really a great guy.

Erika: Trust me, I've known him a lot longer than you have and I know him more than he knows himself. So everything you have to say about him, I've already told him myself.

Stacey: I respect that. So, girl-to-girl, how can I get him to break out of that shell of his?

Erika: Can't tell you.

Stacey: Why?

Erika: (She chuckles) Honestly, girl-to-girl, (She changes her expression to being serious) I just don't trust you. Becky is a bad influence and I don't like being around people with bad influences. D is like my family and I'm not watching him get hurt again. You want to be with him? Prove it to me first.

Stacey: If you care for him so much, then why aren't the two of you together?

Erika: (She takes a sip of her drink) I have my reasons.

Stacey: But you don't trust me enough to say?

Erika: Exactly.

Stacey: All right. How can I prove it to you?

Erika: Be there for him that's all. Just don't B.S. That just pisses me off more that it does him.

Stacey: I can do that.

Erika: Just know that if you ever cheat on him or even dream of doing him wrong, (She pauses) let's not worry about that now. Just understand that it took him years to become what he is, but he's still a little fragile inside. (She slowly walks up to her) Know this; I am going to personally make sure that you're good enough for him. If I ever find out that you've been teaming up with tricks like Becky. It's going to get a lot more physical between us. So don't try to break D's heart, you got it? You break that, I break you.

Stacey: I don't want to do that and I won't.

Erika: (She quickly steps back with a grin on her face) Goodie! You're on the right track so far. Just keep it up and everything will be fine.

Stacey: I know it will. So tell me, how did the group meet?

Erika: It was back in middle school, and we all had a class together. I met D after some kids were beating him up. Then later, we met the others. D was the only one who got kicked out more than anyone on that class. At least until high school.

Stacey: What did he do?

Erika: D and one of his friends were messing around until D pulled out some staple gun staples and shot it from between his teeth. It missed his friend and got the teacher in the eye.

Stacey: Oh my god.

Erika: I know. When he got back, he seemed so different. He talked more and we learned he has a great sense of humor. Since then we've been friends since.

Stacey: That wasn't the end of it was it?

Erika: Nope. Throughout the remaining years, D has still never failed to shock and amaze with his antics.

Stacey: You say that as if he wasn't always happy.

Erika: He wasn't.

Stacey: How was he before?

Erika: Sad, angry, and always felt that his life was meaningless. There were times that he attempted to end his life on a daily basis. It took years for him to finally shake it off, but small hints of that past still lingers around. That's why he's still a little delicate most of the time.

Stacey: That why you are so overprotective of him?

Erika: No. We have a lot in common. We grew so close that he actually called me the sister he always wanted other than his own, but if he had that when he was younger he wouldn't feel so much pain inside. From that day on, we've been the best of friends always looking out for one another.

Stacey: Is he the same way?

Erika: Only of me. Whenever he gets the sight of something bad about happen to or around me, it's not a pretty sight. He's not like that around someone he's dating though. He gives them the respect of independence and space. He doesn't want get to close enough to where he'll get hurt again. (From behind the house the two hear a fence opening and footsteps followed by a loud conversation. Erika and Stacey look to see who it is. It's D walking with some skater and gothic kids. They all talk and laugh)

Gothic Kid: Dude, that was some tight dancing man.

Skater kid: Hell yeah. You parting with us again soon?

Deshawn: For sure. Get back at me on Friday and we'll do it.

Gothic kid: All right, later D. (The two kids walk back to the backyard and D walks in between Erika and Stacey. He looks at the two in slight confusion)

Deshawn: Got a little distance between the two of you I see.

Erika: Hey D.

Stacey: Hi.

Deshawn: Is everyone gravy?

Erika: As always, but I don't think she's hip to your terminology though.

Deshawn: Oh that's right. I'm sorry. I use gravy to say cool. People tend to pick up what I mean when they're around me for a while like the ever so lovely Erika here.

Stacey: I see. Do you always have a different word for something?

Deshawn: Always. How else am going to keep shocking the world?

Stacey: Duly noted.

Deshawn: (He goes from a smile to looking serious) Wait. (He looks at the two again) Girl talk. Sorry. I'll just come back later.

Erika: That's okay. We were already done talking. Aren't we Stacey?

Deshawn: You sure?

Stacey: Just as she said.

Deshawn: All right. If both sides agree that's all right with me. (He looks to Stacey) Did you want to stay longer or call it a night?

Stacey: I guess we can call it a night. Can you walk me back to the dorms?

Deshawn: Sure. (He walks to Erika) Erika, as always, it has been more than pleasure to kick it with you. (They give each other a hug)

Erika: Likewise. (Erika looks to Stacey for a moment and lowers her head into Deshawn's shoulder) You're going to call me when you get up right? (They let go)

Deshawn: (He steps back and Stacey holds onto his arm) First thing.

Erika: All right. (She rubs his head) You two be safe.

Deshawn: Always. Until tomorrow. (Deshawn and Stacey walk away and Erika watches them for a moment. She takes another sip of her beer and walks back inside) So did you have fun?

Stacey: Yes I did. Thank you.

Deshawn: That's good. (He looks up to the sky) Looks like it's going to rain.

Stacey: I'm in no hurry, plus I like it when it rains. So did you drink?

Deshawn: I would've, but I had to be a good boy tonight.

Stacey: You do that normally?

Deshawn: Drink? Sometimes, only in small increments though. I don't like over-doing it. Too many bad hangovers.

Stacey: I meant being a good boy.

Deshawn: Oh that. Always. People think I'm a lot better sober and refuse to let me get plastered at parties. Unfortunately that leads to me being designated driver to a bunch of flat out drunk frat boys who believe that leaving butt prints on nearby windows and getting into fights downtown are called fun.

Stacey: (She laughs) Does that really happen?

Deshawn: Only on a rated PG-13 night. You don't even want to know the rated R version.

Stacey: Wow. So do you know all the groups in this school?

Deshawn: Only the outsiders. Those are like the only ones that I know the most. Every year at school when the new kids would come in, in less than two days they would know who I was. I knew about ninety-five percent of all the gothic and skater kids in whichever school I was in.

Stacey: Mr. Popularity.

Deshawn: Well, that was my name.

Stacey: You feel happy that you still carry that title?

Deshawn: A little bit. It's a little hard to accept still, but I'm getting used to it. It makes me feel happier that so many people here have so much love for me. It's more than I've felt in a long time.

Stacey: What about your parents?

Deshawn: I haven't talked to them in a long time. Not since I first came here.

Stacey: What happened?

Deshawn: After my dad remarried, I always felt that I was being scratched out of the family and he wanted me out. Once I got the hint when I packed up, I took it and left without looking back.

Stacey: Did you try talking to him?

Deshawn: Nope. I can't. Every time I try to pick up the phone I always put it back down. Everyone else here that I have a problem with, I can tell them to kiss my ass. My father is the only one who intimidates me worse than death.

Stacey: Do you two guys get along?

Deshawn: Sometimes. He's the only one I know who can tell me anything about anything I ask him. He the smartest person I've ever known and the most caring too. (He points to her dorm) Here you are.

Stacey: Maybe I can help. Maybe I can help you talk to him again.

Deshawn: I don't think that would work.

Stacey: Trust me on this. Give me one week and I promise you'll be talking without freaking out.

Deshawn: You really think this would work?

Stacey: Of course I do.

Deshawn: What if it doesn't?

Stacey: It will.

Deshawn: I have a question. Are you always this helpful to people you have interests in?

Stacey: What do you mean?

Deshawn: Over the past few days, you've been nothing but kind and sincere to me. I'm just trying to understand if this is an everyday thing.

Stacey: It's one of my bad habits. It's just that I can't stop liking you for some reason. I guess that ever since that first day of class, I've had a strong attraction to you.

Deshawn: (In slight confusion) Really?

Stacey: Really. You're a great person and I like you a lot. I just want you to know that I can understand if you feel like pushing me away if I'm moving too fast. I just can't help it.

Deshawn: Why?

Stacey: I can't explain. You just have this special glow I admire.

Deshawn: Glow? Like a Bruce Leroy last dragon glow? I don't get it?

Stacey: What's there to get? I care about you D. Can't you see that? I don't care about what happened previous.

Deshawn: Then what do you want then?

Stacey: (She holds his chin) You. (She leans in to kiss him, but he pulls back a few steps)

Deshawn: I don't think we should be doing this.

Stacey: Why are you so afraid of me? What is it that you're so scared of?

Deshawn: Look, I know that you've heard stories about my past relationships. If this is an attempt seeing what makes me tick to break it, I already made my promise. I've made the wrong mistakes before and I'm not making them again.

Stacey: Why must you shut everyone that wants to get close to you?

Deshawn: Because I'm not allowing myself to get hurt again. Okay? The reason why I can't let you in is because out of all these years, I finally feel like I can make a real difference and care for someone who cares about me. The more I feel it and the more I want it I feel like I can never be good enough to have it. Every time that I felt happy thinking that someone cares for me as more than a friend, I always get the dirty end of the stick and I'm tired of it. I shut myself out from that feeling because it cost me my life more that once and that's more than enough time needed to quit trying to waste my time on things that don't matter. For the past few days, I've learned that I may have something I never would've thought I could have in a long time. Something I thought I lost.

Stacey: What's that?

Deshawn: Happiness. The more I want to get close, the more I feel that emotion of the one word I can never say.

Stacey: What word would that be?

Deshawn: Nothing important right now. It's just something I don't use loosely.

Stacey: I understand. At least tell me one thing; when you finally realize that this is real, would you run?

Deshawn: (A moment of silence. Deshawn finally replies) Never. (It starts to rain)

Stacey: (Another moment of silence as the two look at each other) So, what happens now?

Deshawn: You know, for the first time in my life, I don't know. It's late. I should be going before this rain gets worse. (He turns to walk away, but Stacey grabs his arm to stop him Deshawn looks down at her holding his arm and then looks into her eyes)

Stacey: Wait. There's one more thing I want to say before you go.

Deshawn: What's that?

Stacey: (She walks closer to him and places her hand on his chest Deshawn looks down) No matter what you've thought about before, you've always had this. (She pats his chest gently) You never needed anyone to give it back. All I'm asking for is a chance to share it with you. I already plan on sharing mine.

Deshawn: Sure, but there's one thing though. (She slowly lowers her head) I already thought about it. (She gently bites her lower lip. Deshawn lifts his head to look at her for a moment. He places his hand on her cheek and caresses it with his thumb. She holds his hand with her eyes closed and they lean in to kiss each other as the rain falls around them, but Deshawn subtly turns his head away so she can kiss his cheek) We should go inside. (The two slowly walk back to her dorm)

CHAPTER 8

───────────── ▼ ─────────────

Deshawn Narrarates: Even to this day, I still can't figure out why the memories I tried so hard to forget keep coming back to me. Irregardless if I feel good or bad, the slightest negative that comes my way would immediately bring back the pain I went through. Some say its mental instability. They might be right, but I think of it as remembering what made me who I am. Controlling my emotions the best way I could keeps me strong. The only down side is, even the strongest man can fall sometimes.

(The next morning Deshawn slowly wakes up. He stretches on the floor of a dorm room he later hears the voice of Stacey calling to him)

Stacey: Good morning. (Deshawn looks to her)

Deshawn: Morning.

Stacey: How are you doing?

Deshawn: A little cramped in my leg, but I'll be fine. What time is it?

Stacey: Almost eight. Thanks for staying over and keeping me company.

Deshawn: Don't sweat it. It was cold and raining down kind of hard.

Stacey: Making sure I was okay?

Deshawn: That was the plan.

Stacey: So what did you dream about?

Deshawn: (He stops for a moment to think) Nothing.

Stacey: You didn't dream anything at all?

Deshawn: Nope.

Stacey: Well why not?

Deshawn: I don't anymore. Sometimes I get a few images here and there, but usually it's nothing.

Stacey: Did you talk to anybody about it?

Deshawn: Never had a reason to. They are nothing but movies. Scenes that you desperately want to be a part of, but can't. I quit dreaming because they never did me any good. Even as a kid, I always wanted something that told me that I had a place in life. Once I realized that I didn't, I stopped. Some things I do dream about though, but then that's when reality kicks in and then I forget it all.

Stacey: How long has this been going on?

Deshawn: (Silence) Too long. I guess it's a learning experience.

Stacey: About what?

Deshawn: Life. Trying to find what I was missing. At times I gave up. Sometimes I still do. I take it you're about to ask me what started all of this in the first place right?

Stacey: Good guess.

Deshawn: Well, it started when I was a kid. I was about seven at the time. My father was always working and my mom thought that just because she has a kid, doesn't mean she has to take care of it. My older sister was the worst case. She was what I like to call a true rebel without a cause. Always fighting without a reason to. She was the type who thought that friends were better than family which left me screwed because I was always left high and dry. I thought I had nothing, so as a youngster I always felt like I was nothing.

Stacey: That's sad.

Deshawn: Tell me about it. I grew up with nobody until I was about twelve, then that's where the real fun began. My parents divorced and I had to live with good old mom. I never thought a child would ever experience a death sentence daily until I first began staying with her. (He has a quick memory of different times his mother had beat him as a child) The fights were tough, but what else could I do? Ever since then I kind of alienated myself from everyone a lot more and became a ghost. I would just fade myself out from everyone and never think anything else. At times, I thought about suicide. At times I still do. I never enjoyed blaming my present on my past, but living the way I did, tells me that payback is a bitch on the rag.

Stacey: Because everyone here cares for you so much.

Deshawn: Basically.

Stacey: How did you stop?

Deshawn: I didn't.

Stacey: Your life must've been pretty hard.

Deshawn: That's only a fraction of it.

Stacey: Keeping it PG?

Deshawn: To an extent.

Stacey: What about the rest of it?

Deshawn: That's another day. Not every morning I wake up remembering these things.

Stacey: You just brush them off.

Deshawn: Most of the time, but as you grow up you understand the term of how the more things change, the more they stay the same. I like change, that's what makes me so different from everyone else. I never liked the idea of being only one thing. That sucks, living life single minded. What about the rest, you know? I always want to experience something else. At least it gives me something interesting to do.

Stacey: And that's what you do best. I would applaud you, but you get that enough.

Deshawn: Appreciation is always welcome.

Stacey: Well then. (She takes her hand from out of her covers and slowly claps to him a few times)

Deshawn: Thank you, (He stretches again as he speaks. He slowly gets up) your applause comforts me.

Stacey: Anytime.

Deshawn: I would bow, but I'm too tired to.

Stacey: Do you plan on staying?

Deshawn: I wish I could.

Stacey: Until next time?

Deshawn: Until next time. (He adjusts his pants and wipes his shirt) Didn't want to get too comfortable.

Stacey: Just playing it safe?

Deshawn: Always. You still have my number right?

Stacey: Kept it in my phone.

Deshawn: Good. The phone's is always on.

Stacey: I will call.

Deshawn: Sooner than later?

Stacey: Give me a few hours.

Deshawn: You got to get fresh and all that, I know.

Stacey: (She scoffs) Look who's talking.

Deshawn: (He sniffs his shirt) Touché. I'll see you. (He closes the door and quickly opens it) Lunch?

Stacey: Sure.

Deshawn: Cool. (He attempts to close the door, but opens it again) In a few hours right?

Stacey: (She laughs) Go.

Deshawn: Just making sure. (He sings) You can call me, call me. We can do something. (Stacey continues to laugh)

Stacey: I will.

Deshawn: Bye.

Stacey: Bye. (Deshawn walks down his dorm hallway thinking to himself as he walks. He stops by his room door and pulls out his phone and looks to it. He searches through his phone book and finds his parents number. He slowly moves his thumb over to the talk button, but stops. He releases a sigh and puts the phone back in his pocket and leans against the wall. A few moments later, Deshawn walks into his room. Jose wakes up out of his sleep and notices him entering the room)

Jose: 'Sup man.

Deshawn: What's going on?

Jose: Where you been?

Deshawn: Chilling with Stacey. She felt sick on the way back to her dorm, so I stayed to make sure she was all right.

Jose: You lay the pipe down?

Deshawn: Hell no. She wasn't ready, (They laugh) besides, I kind of like her. Nothing serious or anything.

Jose: You sure?

Deshawn: Of course.

Jose: Just making sure. I may be half sleep, but I still remember that look.

Deshawn: What look?

Jose: That dumb ass one on your face right now. The look you always have whenever you're thinking about getting serious with someone.

Deshawn: Could you describe it please?

Jose: Like you're in a different zone. Happily, you're not the type that mentions the girls' name in every conversation. All you do is sit there cheesing like the Joker from Batman.

Deshawn: Oh shut it up. I could never like a girl that much. Not anymore anyway.

Jose: Praise Jesus.

Deshawn: What's on deck for today?

Jose: (Yawning) Don't know. You talk to Erika yet?

Deshawn: Not yet. I was about to get cleaned up first before I call her.

Jose: (He rolls over in his bed) Don't use up all the hot water.

Deshawn: Don't worry, I will. (He walks into the bathroom and takes off his shirt. He looks at himself in the mirror for a moment and looks to his wrist. He stares at the scars on his wrist. He lowers his hand and walks in the shower as he turns the water on. He has flashbacks of himself as a child placing a knife to his arm and blood slowly dripping out. The steam mildly rises around him and voices flood his mind)

Young boy: Why don't you just kill yourself and get it over with?

Young boy #2: God, you're such a loser.

Young girl: I don't know what his problem is, but he needs some serious help.

Mother: I want a divorce.

Father: I want to be with my son.

Deshawn: Why can't I get rid of you?

(Next flashback is of Erika sitting with him in a school cafeteria in their younger days. Deshawn lays his head on the table as Erika sits close to him)

Erika: Is everything okay?

Deshawn: I can't do this anymore. Living every single day like it's my first instead of my last. Why can't I be happy even for a moment? Instead I live like this.

Erika: You'll be fine, quit worrying about these things so much.

Deshawn: That's just it, I can't. Everything's fine here away from home. (His eyes become watery) I don't want to go back there.

Erika: Did she hurt you again?

Deshawn: Always. (He wipes the tears from his eyes)

Erika: Are you still on the medication?

Deshawn: No. My dad said not to.

Erika: What does your dad say?

Deshawn: He said that I don't need drugs to make myself feel happy. So I stopped taking them, but the hardest part for him to understand is that if I shouldn't take them to feel happy, then what do I have left that will?

Erika: You have us. You also have me. (She takes a paper napkin from her lunch tray and slowly hands it to him as she speaks softly to him) Here.

Deshawn: (Sniffs) Thank you.

Erika: How's your niece?

Deshawn: Beautiful as always. She's walking a little bit now. I'm pretty much the closest thing she has to a father.

Erika: Your sister still acting up?

Deshawn: As always. It's an everyday thing with her. Makes me wish sometimes that you can take her place.

Erika: Wishes can come true for some people. (She holds his arm and slowly moves it towards her. Deshawn gently winces and pulls his arm back) Can I ask you to promise me something? Please, no more reminders. I don't want you doing this to yourself anymore. Can you do that? For me?

Deshawn: I want to so badly, but it's so hard to for me to. It's hard to forget. I don't want remember anymore.

Erika: I don't want you to either, but I don't want to find out that you forgot by giving yourself more of these. (She gently taps his arm) When did you do this?

Deshawn: Yesterday.

Erika: Why didn't you tell me?

Deshawn: I couldn't. I was too scared to.

Erika: You don't have to be scared anymore. If your mom hurts you again, you tell me okay?

Deshawn: Okay. (The school bell rings and Deshawn snaps out of his flashback. He turns on the shower and steps inside. He stands in the middle in the water with his eyes open as he thinks to himself. "Do good things really come to those who wait? What about the ones who lack the patience to? What becomes of them? Can I finally be happy after all of these years? I can't allow myself to fall into disbelief. No more reminders." Moments later the phone rings. Deshawn walks out of the bathroom wearing a wet towel and answers it) Hello. (Erika answers)

Erika: Good morning D.

Deshawn: Good morning.

Erika: What are you doing?

Deshawn: What are you doing?

Erika: Waking you up stupid.

Deshawn: Well, you're a little bit late. I was already up.

Erika: I was about to have lunch, when are you coming over?

Deshawn: In a minute. I just have to finish getting ready.

Erika: Time?

Deshawn: Give me about thirty minutes.

Erika: Sweet. I'll see you in a little while then.

Deshawn: All right later. (He hangs up the phone and walks to Jose's bed and slaps his arm. Jose quickly rolls around to Deshawn)

Jose: Damn it fool! What?

Deshawn: Get dressed. We're meeting Erika in thirty.

Jose: Wake me up in ten.

Deshawn: Quit lying there looking like a pack of dirty underwear and get up.

Jose: Oh damn it! (He throws the blankets off of himself and gets out of bed. He walks to the shower scratching his head) There better be some hot water left.

Deshawn: (In a southern slave voice) Why yes massa. I'll be sure that the hot water work. (In his normal voice) Just hurry up.

Jose: Ah shut up. (Jose closes the door)

CHAPTER 9

▼

Deshawn Narraration: I get asked every now and again, why am I so much of a vicious bastard when it comes to how I treat women? It's from what I've learned about them. Besides, once you start going broke from spending so much money on them, I think that qualifies as a good reason to be one.

(Time passes, Deshawn and his friends sit at a small diner and talk)

Quinn: So what happened last night?

Jose: Yeah, inquiring minds want to know.

Deshawn: Not much really. Stacey was getting cold from all the rain and I opted to stay at her spot to make sure she was all right. Nothing happened. All I did was sleep on the floor.

Erika: You stayed at her place?

Deshawn: Yeah.

Erika: All night?

Deshawn: Yeah.

Erika: And nothing happened?

Deshawn: Nope.

Erika: That's good. Well, at least we know that she's not a ho.

Deshawn: True.

Quinn: (He quickly cuts in) Wrong! Let me get this straight, you stayed the night with a girl and you did nothing? Why didn't you do something when you were lying on the bed?

Deshawn: Maybe because I was sleeping on the floor. Did you forget that I said that?

Quinn: And you didn't even cop a feel? (He places his hand on Deshawn forehead) Are you all right up there?

Deshawn: I'm fine, thank you. (He takes Quinn's hand off his head) I'm not the type that likes to take advantage. I felt that what I did was the right.

Quinn: Right, but you never even felt her up though. Did you at least give her a hug?

Deshawn: Now that, I did.

Jose: When was this?

Deshawn: When we standing in the rain.

Jose: And you were doing?

Deshawn: Keeping her warm, remember? It was cold and raining. Is any of this clicking yet?

Quinn: (He thinks for a moment) Nope it don't.

Erika: At least nothing happened. That's the most important thing. Keeping your knob away from loose women. I'm proud of you D.

Deshawn: Thank you. See that? Someone here has the kindness and decency to understand where I coming from. Thank you Erika.

Quinn: Look, I'm going to speak my piece for a minute here okay? So far, this girl really digs you for the time being. As a man you are entitled to one free test run to decide if this is a good thing for you. As your friend, I am giving you permission to. (He pounds on the table with his fist. Erika puts her hand on top of his to stop him)

Erika: There's no need for all of that, thank you.

Quinn: (He points his finger at her) Shut up woman, I'm talking here. So you're just going to have to wait your turn.

Erika: (She grabs his finger) Look douche bag, you need to stop before this finger goes treasure hunting up your ass. (She lets go and looks to Deshawn) D, don't mind him right now.

Quinn: Why can't I speak to the boy?

Erika: Because you'll do nothing, but confuse him. No more nonsense or I make sure you have no more balls. (She looks to Deshawn) D, listen to me now. (Quinn moves behind her and mimics her talking with his hand) I want you to understand that what you are doing is good. You are showing that you're still a good person. (She stops for a moment. She quickly turns to Quinn. When she does, Quinn looses his balance sitting on his chair and falls to floor. The group laughs) You see that? If you keep listening to him, you'll wind up being stupid. Do you wanna be an accident prone pimp? Is that what you want D?

Deshawn: A little bit, except without the accident prone part though.

Erika: (She slaps him in his head) No, stupid. Listen, if you think that this Stacey is a good girl, then keep it slow. None of that fast crap all right? If you really like her let her know, but keep it simple. None of that stuff you use to do, okay?

Deshawn: Like what?

Jose: Ah hell, here we go. One: the very expensive engagement ring.

Erika: Not to mention the tennis bracelet.

Quinn: Or the cases they came in.

Erika: And a hard to find autographed poster of a rap star.

Deshawn: All right I get it! So I was a little bit spend thrifty with the ladies, but so what, I was young and stupid at the time.

Jose: Sometimes still stupid.

Deshawn: Hush up peasant boy! Look I know what I'm doing. I'm not going back into what I used to do okay? I am officially the relationship turtle. I'm taking it as slow as possible. Not too fast, but not too slow either.

Erika: Well put. Keep it that way.

Quinn: Hell yeah. Go cheap on her. Get her a friendship ring or something. Ten dollars, you're done. If she leaves, what are you going to do, keep the receipt on a cheap piece of glass?

Jose: Exactly, nothing says loving, like something from the dollar store.

Deshawn: Yeah, you should know. You go there everyday.

Jose: Hell yeah! At least I'm never broke. Twenty dollars a week and I'm living like a king.

Deshawn: Good point. Maybe I'll do that.

Jose: (He slams the table) That's what I'm talking about. So when are we going?

Deshawn: We aren't. I was joking.

Jose: Okay, but you will learn soon enough. Yes you will.

Erika: Pay no mind to these idiots here. Look here's what you do, get her a card first. If things go right, then come to me first and I'll tell you where to go from there. Cool?

Deshawn: Fine with me.

Quinn: You're going to take her side?

Deshawn: She's making sense. I'm sorry, but she's got a point. Test the waters first and if the tide is right, surf.

Jose: (Confused) What? (He looks to Quinn) Can I hit him please? (Quinn shrugs his shoulders. Before Jose can attempt to hit him, Erika punches him in the side of his stomach. Jose quickly holds his side in pain)

Erika: Thanks for the opening stupid. I hate to say it, but looks like you two lost this battle.

Quinn: We'll see. Just remember what we told you. Erika, the boy will come around. (He looks to D) D, trust us and you will succeed.

Erika: I got an idea. Why don't you just buy her a friendship ring? Think about it, no commitments and no ties. That way, you can never feel like you're too attached. That way if anything ever happens, you'll never lose out on anything.

Quinn: True. Just get her a cheap-ass ring. Cost's you about three or four dollars anyway.

Erika: (She throws a plastic spoon at him and points) Don't even think about trying to trap him in your fat web of cheapness. A woman should be given a little more appreciation and be treated with a little more respect.

Quinn: Yeah, but a ho shouldn't.

Jose: He's got a point. D damn near went broke with all the money he spent on the hookers he's been with. We don't know Stacey's true intentions, nor do we know her for that matter. So why should he even bother with worrying about how to treat her yet? (Deshawn thinks about what Jose is saying) What if he gets her the decent ring and she turns about to be flakey? What then? You made a good point about the friendship ring though? All I'm saying is that until we know where her place is, D should keep her where she is now until we know the deal with her, let alone him.

Deshawn: There's nothing wrong with my judgment.

Jose: No, there's just a problem with your reaction with it. All a woman has to do is say that she wants you in the right way and then you turn to jell-o. This time, we want to know before you do.

Deshawn: And you will. I'm not going to hide anything from you guys all right? I'll do this, I'll get two rings.

Quinn: What?!

Deshawn: Let me finish, I'll get one that good and one that's cheap. I'll wait for the right moment to decide and when I do (He looks to the group) I bring the expensive one back.

Quinn: That's what I'm talking about. You're learning boy. I like that.

Deshawn: Taking notes the entire time.

Quinn: (He looks to Erika) And you thought we were doing him wrong.

Erika: You got lucky. I'll give you that one.

Deshawn: I got to admit it though, all of you are helping a lot. Jose you're right, I really do fall to quick for things without thinking them through. Quinn, I do feel like a retarded prostitute and just throw all of my money away to keep my so-called pimps happy. Erika, you are definitely right, take things as slow as possible and don't fall too quick for the tricks. Q and Jose, let's go get the cheap stuff and Erika, I'll get with you about getting the good stuff to buy. Is that cool with everybody?

Erika: Fine with me.

Jose: Cool.

Quinn: I'm down for it.

Deshawn: All right. Let's go shopping. (They all get up from their seats and walk out. Meanwhile, Stacey walks around her room searching for things to wear for the day when her phone begins to ring. She looks around for a moment and digs through a small pile of her clothes until she finally finds it. She presses the answer button and quickly puts the phone to her ear and answers)

Stacey: Hello. Hi, Becky.

Becky: (She leans against a wall in a dorm hallway while on her phone) What are you doing?

Stacey: Not much really. Just (She looks around her mildly unorganized room for a second) a little quick spring cleaning.

Becky: Quick spring cleaning? You are aware of what the current season situation is right? (Before Stacey can respond, Becky replies) Listen, me and the girls are going to go shopping later on. You want to go?

Stacey: Well, sure.

Becky: Goody, I'll be there in a second. (She hangs up her phone and puts it in her purse. She adjusts her hair and pauses for a second. She looks to her left and knocks on the door next to her. Inside the room, Stacey quickly looks to the door and walks to it. She opens the door and its' Becky staring at her with a small smile on her face. Stacey looks in slight confusion as she looks to her phone, then to Becky) Knock, knock. You ready?

Stacey: (She sounds unsure) Yeah.

Becky: Are you sure because it sure doesn't sound like it.

Stacey: (She shakes her head for a second) I'm sorry. I was just a little shocked.

Becky: If we are going to be friends, you are going to have to learn to be a little more on point and be ready for any outing that we are going to have.

Stacey: I'm sorry.

Becky: (She looks to see what Stacey is wearing) Well, it's a good thing that we're going shopping. You are in dire need of a fashion upgrade. (She lifts her hand to her) Let's go. (Stacey takes her hand and walks out the door. Stacey closes the door and locks it with her free hand. The two walk away) So, how are things with you and D?

Stacey: Good, real good.

Becky: Well, I'm happy for the both of you.

Stacey: You're not still mad at him?

Becky: Not really. I have learned that time heals all wounds. I have decided to just do what I can to get D to understand that I want to start over with a clean slate and forget what happened.

Stacey: You sound like a bible salesman.

Becky: I know. I've begun to outgrow all of this constant negativity between us. I only want to end all of this childish madness before it gets worse.

Stacey: Quite the insight.

Becky: (Chuckles) Tell me about it. I just wish there was some way to get him to understand what it is that I want to do. Telling him in person only makes it worse.

Stacey: I could tell him for you.

Becky: (She stops) Really? You would do that for me?

Stacey: Well, sure. How hard could it be? We basically talk all the time. I could bring it up to him if you want?

Becky: I would really appreciate it if you did that.

Stacey: It's no problem. It's the least I could do for a friend.

Becky: (They continue walking) Thanks. So how's school going?

Stacey: Very well. (As they walk through the hallway, a few of the boys stare at her. She smiles with her head down and adjusts her hair)

Becky: Becoming quite the sight as well I see.

Stacey: A little bit.

Becky: Not to worry. After today, you will be the most sought after girl in this dorm.

Stacey: I don't know. I enjoy spending time with D. I don't want to just start chasing after other guys.

Becky: You won't have to. They come to you.

Stacey: I've noticed. It's a good thing I don't go up on their offer too.

Becky: Why is that?

Stacey: Think about it. If I go out with them instead of D, then everything that he said in class on my first day will be true.

Becky: You actually remembered what he said in class and you're referring him as D? You must really like him.

Stacey: I do.

Becky: So hold up. You really are serious about dating him?

Stacey: I am. He's really a great guy.

Becky: I guess I can understand that. There are other fish in the sea you know. Why prevent yourself from even talking to one of these guys?

Stacey: I've seen their type before, using their ego and expensive clothing to think that everything is theirs for the taking. I'm just not into that type of thing.

Becky: Not all of these guys are like that.

Stacey: Really? Name one person that isn't like that.

Becky: I can name a lot.

Stacey: From where?

Becky: That's for later on.

Stacey: Wait a second. I have to meet with D tonight.

Becky: You will. Call it a pit stop. I have to meet with him to go over a few things it'll only take a minute. (They walk outside towards the school parking lot)

Stacey: I have to let D know. (She pats her pockets) I left my phone in my room. Can I use yours?

Becky: I didn't bring mine.

Stacey: Didn't you call me from my door?

Becky: I used someone else's. One of the many perks of being popular. Besides, you can call him later after we're finished.

Stacey: What all are we doing?

Becky: Do I have to have a reason to want to hang out with you? If I did, I would not have called in the first place.

Stacey: I'm sorry. So, where are we going to first?

Becky: First, the mall, then we eat and chill for a little while.

Stacey: That's cool. You're sure that this won't take long right?

Becky: Trust me. (They walk to her car. Becky pulls out her keys from her purse and unlocks the door and both get in. At that moment, Deshawn pulls up on the parking lot not too far from Becky. Quinn catches a quick glimpse and points from inside. He thinks for a moment and looks to Jose. He mouths to him)

Quinn: Isn't that Stacey?

Jose: What? (He looks out the window and sees her from the back window getting into Becky's car)

Quinn: Was that her?

Jose: I don't know. Maybe.

Quinn: Aren't they supposed to be doing something today?

Jose: Yeah.

Quinn: Then why is she with her?

Jose: How the hell should I know?

Quinn: You going to tell D?

Jose: No. We don't even know what's going on. If something happens, then we step in, but for now don't worry about it.

Deshawn: (He cuts in) Why do you two look like you're about to kiss each other back there? Ya'll got something to tell me?

Jose: (He grabs his crotch) Kiss these.

Deshawn: Sorry, but I left my microscope back in the room.

Quinn: (He laughs) D's got jokes.

Deshawn: And you've got crabs. (He parks at a nearby spot in the parking lot) Now that we're back, does this conclude the day or kick it longer?

Erika: I'll stay.

Jose: I'm cool with it.

Quinn: (He quickly responds) Before we go back out, I got to speak to Jose for a quick minute.

Jose: (He looks in confusion) About what?

Quinn: About the stuff we were talking about earlier.

Jose: What?

Quinn: Just open the door.

Jose: Fine. I'll see you later.

Deshawn: All right peace. (Jose and Quinn exit the car. Deshawn looks to Erika) I think that boy's got issues.

Erika: You just now noticed? Let's go get this ring.

Deshawn: Yes mother. Before we go, there's something that I have to do first. (He puts the car in reverse and slowly pulls out. Meanwhile, Quinn leads Jose inside the dorm. Jose looks down in thought)

Quinn: Good they're gone.

Jose: May I ask a question? (He stops to look to Quinn) Just what the hell was all that about?

Quinn: To ask you in my normal tone of voice about what the hell we just saw.

Jose: Wait, hold it. Just chill out and calm down all right. I already explained my self in the car.

Quinn: On what? We have to sit and do nothing while Stacey gets brainwashed by Satan's love child?

Jose: Look, I told you before, we don't even know what's going on with the two of them. So for right now, we can't say anything about what we saw until we know for sure what's up.

Quinn: Then what ways do we have to make for sure. The girl won't tell us, then who will she talk to.

Jose: (He looks up and sees Kevin talking to some of the football players as they toss a ball around) The two for one special. (He walks towards Kevin. Quinn follows beside him)

Quinn: Say what?

Jose: Kevin. If he can't help us find out what's going on from Becky, then you know for sure that everyone else who knows her will.

Quinn: That's a good idea.

Jose: By doing this, we don't risk playing the instigators. All we're doing is getting info and that's it.

Quinn: So then what if Becky is doing something fowl?

Jose: Not focused on that right now. (They walk up to Kevin) 'Sup Kevin.

Kevin: What's going on?

Jose: Not much really. I have a question for you though, more like a request of a small favor.

Kevin: What's up?

Jose: We have this situation.

Kevin: Which would be?

Quinn: We think Becky's planning something foul with D and we need your help with figuring out what's going on.

Kevin: Sure. I don't know how much I can do, but I'll try.

Jose: Thanks man.

Kevin: What might be the problem?

Jose: We saw Stacey with her not to long ago and just to be safe, we want to make sure that nothing is going on for D's sake.

Kevin: Cool. I'll ask around and see what's up. If I find anything I'll let you know.

Jose: Cool. We'll see you later. (Quinn and Jose walk away)

CHAPTER 10

▼

Deshawn Narrarates: Some say that the best way to put the past behind you, is to go to where it all started. For me, it's my own family. My mother and sister left a long time ago and my dad remarried and has a daughter. The hardest part about this is either I get the feeling of tough love coming or the feeling of being replaced. Either one I get, I'm not ready for.

(Later on that day, Deshawn pulls into a driveway in front of a large house. He cuts off the engine and looks at the house. Erika looks to him)

Erika: It's been a long time since you've been here.

Deshawn: I know.

Erika: You sure you're going to be okay?

Deshawn: Doubt it.

Erika: Want me to go with you?

Deshawn: (He sighs) Unfortunately for me, this is one of those things that I have to do alone.

Erika: (She pats on gently on the back of the neck and slowly rubs it) Be careful okay?

Deshawn: To see him again? I'm going to need a hell of a lot more than that to get through this. (He looks to Erika) Wish me luck.

Erika: You'll do fine. I'll go out with you and stay outside the door, okay?

Deshawn: Thanks. Here we go. (The two get out of the car and walk to the door. Deshawn tries to knock on the door, but hesitates. He has another flashback of him as a child sitting next to his father on a bed. The younger Deshawn hugs a pillow close to him. Without looking at him, his father says to him)

Dad: I want you to go somewhere with me tomorrow.

Younger Deshawn: Where are we going?

Dad: Don't worry about where we're going. I just want you to go with me some-place.

Younger Deshawn: Ok. I'm gonna go to bed. Good night daddy.

Dad: Good night. (The next morning, younger Deshawn is in the back seat of his parents' car as they drive through the city. They stop at a tall building and park. The family all step out of the car and walks towards the building. Later that day, Deshawn is sitting in a chair surrounded by other children in hospital robes talking about their problems. Younger Deshawn gets out of his chair and walks to one of the nurses. As he does he remembers his parents' words)

Mother: We'll be back for you in a little bit ok?

Younger Deshawn: Where are you going?

Mother: We just have to go take care of some things. Just wait here ok?

Younger Deshawn: Ok mamma. (The voices stop as younger Deshawn does once he reaches the nurse) Excuse me. When will my parents come back for me?

Nurse: They want you to stay here with us for a little while ok? Everything's fine.

Younger Deshawn: But it's dark outside and my mommy and daddy aren't here yet.

Nurse: They'll be coming back for you soon it's ok. Just have a seat with the other kids. You're family will be back before you know it ok? (Younger Deshawn is unresponsive as the flashback ends and the older Deshawn still standing in front of the door. Erika slowly walks up behind him)

Erika: What's wrong?

Deshawn: Back to the drawing board.

Erika: What? What are you thinking about?

Deshawn: How all of this began. My first feeling of betrayal and I wasn't even nine. Remember the time where I told you about when my parents told me that I had to go somewhere with them one day and it turned out to be an institution for kids? They told me they would be right back. I didn't know it was gonna be after Christmas and New Years'. After that, there were countless counselors and therapists. Everyone at school got more of a reason to kick me around and no one gave a damn. They say all of it was to make me better, but a lot of good that did.

Erika: D? Listen to me and listen to me good. You're my best friend and you're the only one who's closest to me. Accomplishing a feat like that is really hard to do. So that says enough.

Deshawn: You're right. (Erika watched him with concerned eyes and slowly places her hand on his)

Erika: Hey, you don't have to do this if you don't want to.

Deshawn: I don't want to, but I have to. Gotta stop running sometime. (He knocks on the door. Moments later, the door opens and a little girl stands in the doorway. She looks to Deshawn and yells)

Little Girl: Big brother! (She quickly hugs him tightly and Deshawn hugs her back) I missed you!

Deshawn: I missed you too munchkin. (The little girl looks to Erika)

Little Girl: Hi Erika.

Erika: Hey Jaime! How have you been little one?

Jaime: Fine. (She looks at Deshawn) Mom and dad are here.

Deshawn: (He looks to Erika with a mild smile on his face) Great. (The two walk inside. Jaime closes the door and jumps in front of the two)

Jaime: Mama is sleep and Dad is in the living room.

Deshawn: (He whispers) Wonderful.

Erika: (She hears him and pats him on the back. She looks to him and she whispers as well) Hey, you're going to be fine.

Deshawn: Tell him that. (A man's voice speaks from the living room)

Man: Jaime. Who's at the door?

Jaime: It's big brother. (Erika watches Deshawn walk into the living room and leans against the wall. Deshawn sees his father sitting on the couch and stands close to the wall behind him with his hands behind his back)

Deshawn: Hey dad.

Dad: Hi. What's up?

Deshawn: Not much, just wanted to see how you were doing that's all.

Dad: We're doing okay. Your grandparents are over at the V.A.

Deshawn: Are they doing okay?

Dad: Yeah. I've been meaning to ask you, what was the deal with you smoking before you left?

Deshawn: Dad, that was a year ago.

Dad: I know. Before you left almost every morning there would be nothing, but cigarette butts all over the outside of the driveway out there. What was that about?

Deshawn: You're bringing this up now?

Dad: Yeah. Don't nobody in this house smoke except for your uncle and he does all that craziness out in the back.

Deshawn: I know, but why are you bringing this up now?

Dad: Why can't you answer the question?

Deshawn: Because.it's been over a year and the only thing that you can ask me is not "how have you been", but "why were you smoking at the house last year"?

Dad: As long as you've been in this house, it's been almost nothing, but a mad house. You staying out all hours not telling anyone in here where you been. You smoking and hanging around all these wood heads and carrying on. What if something happened to you? You don't tell nobody nothing in this house like we're out to get you or something like that.

Deshawn: Nothing did happen to me.

Dad: What if it did? Did you ever think about that? Like I said, you don't tell nobody anything about what you're doing. Walking around like some kind of stranger who just lives here. Everyday it was the same thing; I ask you, where are you going? The only thing you say was "out to go meet with your friends" and go on out the door.

Deshawn: Well, I'm sorry, but I haven't had any friends since we first moved to this place. So I apologize if that was a new thing for me.

Dad: We're supposed to be your family and you just treated it like that wasn't important.

Deshawn: It was important. If it wasn't then why didn't I end up like my sister? Haven't you ever thought about that?

Dad: I don't need to think about that. She isn't here is she? She's the one that ran off and thought nothing else about us. She's the one who took Renee and just disappeared. Now you take that and everything else that I have to do around here and tell me if I'm supposed to go out of my way to stress about what she did?

Deshawn: I guess not, but what about Renee? Is she a part of this whole stress relief thing that you do too? Is she not important either?

Dad: She is important.

Deshawn: Then why didn't you do anything to help her? I've busted my backside trying to do everything I could to find her while you did nothing.

Dad: Say if you do find her. Then what? She won't even remember you.

Deshawn: At least she would know that I loved her enough where she is. I cared for that little girl ever since she was first born. I loved her to the point where I would call her my own daughter and the only thing that you can tell me is still to leave her be?

Dad: I know it's hard, but that's how things are.

Deshawn: (He gets a little louder) Why does it have to be like this? Why is it that every time something special happens to me I lose it? Then the only thing that you have to say is just to forget about it. Just like everything else right? Constantly comparing me to my uncle and my sister. Forcing me to forget about the only thing that made me happy in my useless life. Treating me like I would never be enough to be a part of this family and not to mention never being able to stay on the subjects of what we talk about. Always stopping once I make sense and trying to jump to something else that has no value over what we're discussing.

Dad: That's because I'm trying to get you to understand the real differences between right and wrong. You remember when your mother put me out? What was the first thing that she thought was supposed to happen to me? I was supposed to be out half dead on the street with all them other winos and crack heads. Instead I did what I wasn't ready to do yet, I picked myself right back up and brought us here. I wasn't ready for it, but I had to do it anyway. I busted my backside to prove to her that she wasn't going to beat me and as long as I'm alive, nobody will. That was one of the many lessons I've been trying to teach you. Life is never easy. There's always gonna be somebody that wants to step on what you got. I kept telling you that the greatest revenge is massive success. All of these riff raffs around here think that they can make it by trying to duck and dodge everything. Then, the time you take to do different and succeed in doing what you want to do, you'll see. All of them people that you normally hang around with, are still going to be doing the same thing, working the same jobs and when they see you being successful then they'll start trying to milk you for what you have. Try to get back to being buddy-buddy with you when all they want got nothing to do with you, but what you got in your pocket.

Deshawn: I know, you tell me all of the time. I keep trying to tell you that I'm not going to end up like them. I know what I want to do and I know where I want to go. Why do you keep thinking that I'm never going to amount to anything?

Dad: I never said that.

Deshawn: But you keep giving me the impression.

Dad: Then why do you always have this attitude like everyone is against you?

Deshawn: I don't know.

Dad: You do know. All everyone in this house has tried to do was help you. Then it seems like every time we do, you go off in this rebel mode and start doing stuff only crazy people do. And I know it's stuff you're not supposed to be doing because your sister used to do the same thing.

Deshawn: (Under his breath) This is so dumb.

Dad: Every time we try to help her, she would run off with her friends and get into all kinds of wild nonsense. Then get mad at us when we try to get her to stop. All we've ever tried to do was help you out.

Deshawn: I understand that dad, but what I don't understand is why is it that every time we get into discussions like this, or anyone for that matter, you always have to compare me to either my sister or someone else in the family. How many times do I have to explain to you that I have nothing to do with them? I swear, it's like every time that we talk about anything, you always blame stuff that has nothing to do with me on me. Everything that I have an interest in, it automatically becomes the reason why I was so depressed and now this stuff. That's okay. I understand what it is that you want to do. All of these years of not telling me, but showing it, I understand now.

Dad: Understand what?

Deshawn: That you don't want me to be a part of this family. All of this pushing me to the side, I get it now. Ever since I got out of high school, better yet before then, you have done nothing, but cast me aside. Almost as if you're trying to prove to me how much I don't belong in this family anymore. You want me gone? Fine. I don't need this shit. Erika let's go. (He quickly walks towards the door and Erika follows. Deshawns' father starts to walk after him)

Dad: Deshawn, don't you walk out that door.

Deshawn: Too late. (The door slams. Deshawn and Erika continue to walk to the car. Once they get inside, Erika watches Deshawn face. The house door opens and Deshawns' sister runs out)

Jaime: Big brother! (She runs to his window) Where are you going?

Deshawn: Home little sis.

Jaime: When will you come back?

Deshawn: Good question. (Erika leans forward to see Jaime)

Erika: It won't be long. Now come on, give me a hug goodbye. (Jaime runs to Erika's window and gives her a hug) Now you go back inside okay?

Jaime: Okay. Bye big brother. I love you!

Deshawn: I love you too Jaime. (He speak to where only Erika can hear) Can't say the same for some other people in that fucking house. (Deshawn starts the ignition and pulls out of the driveway. As Deshawn drives, Erika looks out of the window in thought)

Erika: Well, that went fairly well.

Deshawn: Yeah, like clockwork.

Erika: I swear, like father, like son.

Deshawn: (He sighs) Here we go. What?

Erika: The two of you put on this rough stone-like shield around you to prevent anyone seeing that you're hurt. Once you do that, you shift into this defensive mode where you either respond with short sentences or say nothing at all.

Deshawn: One of my better traits I got from him.

Erika: Don't forget the fact that both of you are great thinkers. That and you also have great viewpoints on things.

Deshawn: I guess making your child feel like a part of the family wasn't one of them. Help me remember, isn't that one of the things that parents are supposed to know when they have kids?

Erika: (She looks to him) Your dad does love you.

Deshawn: Has a nice way of showing it.

Erika: He really does. From what I can tell, he just wants you to be strong and responsible. Determined to make it on your own, but he's just expressing it differently that other parents would.

Deshawn: That would be by treating me like complete and total ass on a daily basis?

Erika: No, by pushing you into maturity a little bit faster than others. That's probably why you're so much of a deep person the majority of the time. You think and analyze almost everything. You come up with solutions more reasonable than anyone. You make people think and sometimes even change their perspectives on things. I still can't believe that you haven't seen that yet.

Deshawn: Sorry, but when it comes to me and him, I'm too busy being yelled at and compared to everybody else.

Erika: Nobody's perfect. You're his only son. What else do you expect from him?

Deshawn: To be treated like one. Look I respect what you're trying to tell me, but you have to understand that if you want to show your child that you love them, then stop acting like a complete prick and do it. Stop treating me like shit and then afterwards tell me that you're on my side. He's supported me in certain things, this is true, but at the same time, it's like he sets me up for failure. Show your child that you love them, not make them want to throw themselves off a fucking building.

Erika: I know how you feel D. Remember I was with you during all of that stuff with your mom.

Deshawn: Yes and I thank you for that. Stuff like what you do, shows that you actually care. That's what I need. Everyday I felt like my life was meaningless and I needed something more close to me to help get me out of that state of mind. Mainly my family. Unfortunately for me, I had a father like that to show me the wrong way of trying to pull that off.

Erika: Hey. (She holds his hand. Deshawn catches a glimpse in the corner of his eye and looks back to the road) It's going to be all right. Question. You how much I care about you right?

Deshawn: Of course I do.

Erika: Do you think that Stacey can be more than that? (Deshawn is unresponsive. Erika slowly lets go and looks back out of the window. Deshawn pulls into the mall parking lot. As he turns the car off, he responds without looking to Erika)

Deshawn: No one in my life is more important than you. (Erika quickly looks to him) Now let's do this shopping thing. (Before Erika can respond Deshawn gets out of the car. Erika thinks for a moment and gets out of the car as well)

CHAPTER 11

▼

Deshawn Narrarates: The mall is a cluster of a lot of people. stalkers, crazies, nut jobs, kleptomaniac generic thugs looking to prove how hard they are. Let's not forget the young girls who dress like tricks trying to be twenty-one when they're really only thirteen. Pot-smokers, skateboarders, gothic people with wild hair-styles and shiny boots. God, these places are fun to go to. The only thing that isn't are the stores. Countless mini-businesses selling items that you can't afford so all you can do is look and leave. I guess that's all a shopping mall is nowadays. Shopping for Monetary Afflictions or Looking and Leaving. Or just come to meet people because there's nothing else to do. That's mostly what I come here for anyway.

(Erika and Deshawn walk inside a mall and look at the different stores inside. Someone from behind them call out Deshawn's name)

Mike: D! (Deshawn and Erika turn around) What's up man?

Deshawn: Mike! What's going on? (Mike walks up to D in his gothic outfit with chains hanging from his neck and pants) How you been man?

Mike: Good, just checking for some gear to wear.

Deshawn: Still sporting the all black I see.

Mike: My way of living. I see you changed yours. (He gently pulls on his shirt) I still remember when you were wearing stuff like mine for a while. You still working on the music too?

Deshawn: Never miss a day.

Erika: (She raises her hand close to her head and puts it down) Victim of that statement.

Mike: Erika, you look fine as always. A lot of the people we used to hang out with still ask about you two.

Deshawn: We have that effect on people. Are you still planning on those accounting jobs?

Mike: Already got one.

Deshawn: Nice, I told you hiding that brain of yours would do you no good.

Mike: I figured I might as well use it. Better that then mooching off the parents.

Deshawn: Tell me about it. Once I got the chance to come here, I turned into Casper. I was out.

Mike: Speaking of out, (He looks to a nearby store) I got some more shopping to do. I'll catch you guys later cool?

Deshawn: Cool with me.

Mike: All right later. (He runs to the store. Deshawn and Erika keep walking)

Erika: (As she walks, she spots a jewelry store and points to it) See, look. I knew we would find something reasonable to work with.

Deshawn: Lead the way. (They walk into the store and look around) They have some pretty high class style stuff here.

Erika: Not really. They're cheap, reasonable, and more importantly (She looks to Deshawn) just what you need. So what do you think?

Deshawn: I could work with it. (He points to one) What about this one?

Erika: (She looks at it) It's okay.

Deshawn: Not that one then. (He points to another one) Here?

Erika: (She looks at it then to Deshawn) Please, you want to impress her, not insult her.

Deshawn: Sorry, I would get something better, but I left my platinum VISA at home.

Erika: As if you could get one with the bills you're still paying off.

Deshawn: Hey, I'm still good for the next couple of months. (Erika chuckles) How about here? (Erika looks to Deshawn with a serious look, but he doesn't look back at her) Don't say it, moving forward. (He turns to the main display case in the middle of the store. He sees a small silver ring elegantly decorated with a medium sized blue crystal in the middle. He walks to it slowly) Hello Waldo.

Erika: What?

Deshawn: You remember those "Where's Waldo" books growing up?

Erika: How could I forget those junk books? They did nothing, but make you want to throw yourself out a window because they were so aggravating to look at. Why?

Deshawn: Looks like I just found him. (He points to the ring and Erika bends over to look at it. Deshawn notices a tattoo on her lower back)

Erika: Quit staring, it's bad for your health.

Deshawn: I didn't know that looking at your ass can kill? Can it cure Cancer too?

Erika: No, looking at it doesn't. (Without looking, she punches him in his upper thigh and Deshawn quickly falls to the floor) Quit being a baby. It could've been worse. (Deshawn gets up rubbing his hurt leg) Ever since I got that thing, you've been looking at it every chance you got.

Deshawn: What? I like the way it looks. Why do you have to be so violent? (She punches his leg again and Deshawn falls back to the floor. He struggles to get up again) Damn it woman. Do you think that we could try to have a good relationship without all the abuse?

Erika: Love hurts doesn't it?

Deshawn: So, this is your way of showing it?

Erika: Of course. Want me to prove it again?

Deshawn: Please, no.

Erika: All right then. I got to hand it to you though, you sure do have good taste when you want to use it.

Deshawn: Yeah, that and it's the only flashy ring in the middle of the store. That should tell you something about it. What's the price range?

Erika: (She sees the price tag and quickly shields her eyes from it) That's the one. It's too good, even for me.

Deshawn: Are you serious? (He bends down to look at it) Damn! That is good. I'll take it. (He reaches for his wallet. Erika thinks for a second and quickly puts her hand on top of his as he opens his wallet. He looks to her) What?

Erika: (She gently lets go. There is a small moment of silence. Erika then replies) Nothing.

Deshawn: What's wrong?

Erika: Forget it.

Deshawn: Erika, I know when you're pissed off at something. What is it?

Erika: (She becomes defensive) Look, it's nothing all right. Just get the ring and let's go.

Deshawn: Touchy aren't we? You're like the Incredible Hulk with a menstrual cycle.

Erika: It's not that. Forget it. (Deshawn leans on her shoulder and stares at her eyes. She tries not to look. She begins to laugh) Just what are you staring at?

Deshawn: I just wanted to see that smile.

Erika: (She gently moves Deshawn off of her) You really are something else.

Deshawn: It's my gift.

Erika: Let's just get the ring and go.

Deshawn: (He bows to her) As you wish master.

Erika: (She signals him to an associate of the store) Move.

Deshawn: (He reaches in his pocket and looks at his phone for a moment) Weird, I thought Stacey would've called me by now.

Erika: Call her.

Deshawn: I'll wait until later. (Erika stops for a moment and grabs his phone from his pocket and fiddles with it) What are you doing?

Erika: What's it look like? I'm calling her.

Deshawn: (He tries to grab his phone, but Erika pulls her arm away) Give it back.

Erika: No! If you have a question, expect an answer. (She looks at his phone) There she is. (She shows a look of disgust) You already put this chicks picture on your caller id?

Deshawn: I know a lot of chicks with that name. So what?

Erika: You really do suck at lying you know that right?

Deshawn: Well flash that booty more and maybe I'll stop.

Erika: How is flashing my butt going to stop you from lying?

Deshawn: (He thinks for a moment) I don't know, but it sounded smooth. Can I have my phone back please?

Erika: Get back you dork. (She pushes Deshawn back slowly and points at him to signal for him to wait where he is) Hello, Stacey? This is Erika. Yeah, where are you? You were supposed to hang out with D tonight? We're waiting on you. So, you'll call back in a little while. Cool, talk to him later. Bye. (She hangs up the phone) She went out shopping. See, was that so hard?

Deshawn: (He takes his phone from her) Thank you.

Erika: Anytime. Are you still treating me to lunch?

Deshawn: (Confused) Treating you to lunch? When did we agree to that?

Erika: We didn't, I did. Let's go after you pay for that.

Deshawn: Ok. Sure. You're the boss. (They continue to walk to the store employee to talk to him. Later on that day, Deshawn sits in his room with his friends. They all talk and laugh as they listen to rock music. Moments later Deshawn's phone rings. He points to one of his black friends wearing all black clothes) Hey dude, could you pass me my phone please? (His friend moves off his bed and grabs Deshawn's phone and lightly tosses it to him. Deshawn answers it and places the phone to his ear) Hello? What's up Stacey?

Stacey: Hi. I'm sorry about today, it's just that I got so caught up with all this shopping I needed to get done I lost track of time.

Deshawn: It's no big deal. Did you have fun?

Stacey: It would've been a little better if you were here though.

Deshawn: I wish I was with you too.

Stacey: Did you want to get together later on tonight?

Deshawn: Yeah sure. You want me to meet you at your place?

Stacey: I can meet you at yours if that's cool.

Deshawn: That's fine. I'll see you later then.

Stacey: It's a date.

Deshawn: All right bye. (He hangs up the phone. Stacey hangs up the phone. Becky's voice speaks)

Becky: So what did he say? (She sits on the bed with her back against the wall and shopping bags scattered around it)

Stacey: I'm meeting him later on tonight.

Becky: Nice. Before you go, (She digs through one of the shopping bags and pulls out an outfit) you need a good change of clothes. Here. (She tosses them to Stacey)

Stacey: Thanks. You know, I still can't see why D still doesn't like you. You're such a nice person.

Becky: Why, thank you.

Stacey: I think I'll talk to him about that truce you wanted too. (Someone knocks at the door. Becky stands up and walks to the door)

Becky: That is something that I would gladly appreciate. (She opens the door. A tall and handsome black teen stands at the door) Marcus, how are you?

Marcus: I'm good, how about you?

Becky: Just fine. This is Stacey. (She points to her. Stacey and Marcus stare at each other for a moment and Stacey gets up from her chair)

Stacey: I should probably go. I'll see you later. (She walks to the door as she tries to squeeze past Marcus. She lifts her hand to shake his) It was nice meeting you.

Marcus: (He looks at her) Same here. (He shakes her hand and watches her as she leaves. He walks inside the room. As Becky closes the door, she tells him)

Becky: Have I got something to tell you. (She closes the door)

CHAPTER 12

▼

Deshawn Narrarates: The worst part about having enemies is the ones who hate what you've become. Those people will do everything they can to destroy you, no matter what the cost. That poor excuse of menstrual cycle has tried almost every attempt she could to get rid of me. Her plans fail most of the time. Well, actually they all do, but you can't blame someone for trying.

(Later, Stacey walks down a set of stairs as she leaves her dorm. She heads towards the doors of Deshawn's dorm and walks inside. She reaches his room door, but stops to think. The image of Marcus at Becky's door flashes in her head. She then sees Deshawn as he smiles to her. Stacey opens her eyes and looks around. She adjusts her hair and knocks on the door)

Deshawn: (He opens the door just a crack and peeks out) Yes?

Stacey: It's Stacey. Is everything okay?

Deshawn: Of course. How may I be of service?

Stacey: We are supposed to hang out today.

Deshawn: Really? What's the password then?

Stacey: (She laughs) Just open the door.

Deshawn: (He chuckles as he open the door) I'm sorry. Being odd is a force of habit for me.

Stacey: I see that. (She walks inside) So how did your day go?

Deshawn: Fairly well. I did a little shopping.

Stacey: Really, what did you get?

Deshawn: Just some here and there stuff. Nothing fancy. How did your shopping go?

Stacey: It was fun. (She reaches into her purse and takes out a small bag) Here, I got you something while I was out. (Deshawn doesn't respond) Don't look at me like you never received a gift before, Take it.

Deshawn: Sorry, it's just that I'm not used to being given gifts that much. (He looks in the small bag and sees that there is a mood ring inside) A mood ring?

Stacey: It's the thought that counts right? I expect to see bright colors when you're around me ok?

Deshawn: (He response is unsure) Sure. No problem.

Stacey: What's wrong?

Deshawn: Nothing. This is really nice. Thank you. I never got one of these before. (He sets the ring on his desk)

Stacey: Well, this is a good way for me to say that you are special enough to get one.

Deshawn: Thank you. I didn't get you anything.

Stacey: You don't have to. You gave me enough already, so we're even.

Deshawn: Well that can work, (Under his breath) for now at least.

Stacey: Why do you say that?

Deshawn: Say what?

Stacey: That last thing you said.

Deshawn: I didn't say anything.

Stacey: Okay. (She walks over to a chair and sits down) So, did you talk to your parents yet?

Deshawn: Damn, I was hoping you would've forgotten that.

Stacey: I sure didn't. Where's your phone?

Deshawn: In my possession.

Stacey: So that would be where? (Deshawn pats his right pants pocket) So could you remove it from that location please?

Deshawn: Sure. (He reaches into his pocket to get his phone, but stops to think) Is there any place to eat that's open right now? I am really starving right now.

Stacey: That's it. (She hops on his lap and tries to get Deshawn's phone from his pocket. They playfully wrestle for a moment until both fall to the floor. Deshawn rolls on top of her with her arms pinned to the floor. They stare at each other for a moment)

Deshawn: I think I got a cramp in my back. (He rolls off of her and onto his stomach)

Stacey: Aw, poor baby. Here. (She gets on his back and begins to massage him) How's that?

Deshawn: Very nice. If you keep doing that, I may wind up falling asleep.

Stacey: You're going to ask me to come here just so you can fall asleep on me?

Deshawn: I'm just joking.

Stacey: So when are you going to talk to them?

Deshawn: I kinda already did. Didn't go as well as I thought though.

Stacey: Well you can try again. You can do that, can't you? Will you promise me?

Deshawn: Yes, ma'am.

Stacey: I want you to say it.

Deshawn: I just did.

Stacey: No, say that you promise.

Deshawn: All right, I promise with an additional scouts honor. (He holds up two fingers and puts them down)

Stacey: Good job. Can I ask you a question?

Deshawn: Must we go through this again?

Stacey: Why won't you make peace with Becky?

Deshawn: I got tired of trying. (Stacey stops for a second to think)

Stacey: You mean she did?

Deshawn: No, I mean I did. Ever since my first run in with Queen Satan, I've tried nothing but making peace. Every time I've made the attempt, she would set it on fire and dance around it like she was expecting a thunder storm. It got to the point where she tried to turn my own friends against me with her expertise in mind manipulation.

Stacey: So after every attempt you made, you just quit trying.

Deshawn: Not really. I just decided to beat her at my own game instead of hers, which I have successfully proved more than once.

Stacey: How did you do that?

Deshawn: Did what she couldn't, fight my own battles and whoever took my side never needed my persuasion.

Stacey: Same game, but your own rules?

Deshawn: Only way to have it.

Stacey: So, that's why she must dislike you so much.

Deshawn: That's what I heard. I never really bother about what she says about me anyway. Not my problem. The more people worry about others, the less room you have to worry about yourself. That's one of my mottos.

Stacey: Only one?

Deshawn: I got a lot of them.

Stacey: Tell me another.

Deshawn: Never ride on the hood of your friends' car without proper training from a professional stuntman.

Stacey: You did that?

Deshawn: I did a lot of crazy things in my younger days.

Stacey: One more question.

Deshawn: Aim and fire.

Stacey: If I told you that I was beginning to like you more than I am supposed to, what would you say?

Deshawn: (He adjusts his head to where he can hear her a little better) You mean you don't like me anymore?

Stacey: What?

Deshawn: You said "was", as in past tense.

Stacey: You know what I mean.

Deshawn: Actually, I don't.

Stacey: I mean that I am beginning to like you more than I am supposed to. Is that a better way to say it?

Deshawn: Oh, You mean in that way?

Stacey: Yes. That isn't a bad thing, is it?

Deshawn: (He hesitates for a second) Well, no. There's no problem with that. If that's how you feel, than that's nice.

Stacey: Why are you so nervous?

Deshawn: I'm not. It's just that this is fairly quick.

Stacey: You need to learn to catch up if I keep moving fast for you.

Deshawn: You keep sounding like you want some kind of smooth pimp type of guy or something.

Stacey: No, it's just you seem like the type of guy who works with too many restrictions when it comes to relationships. Call it my attempt to drive it out. (She lays on his back and closes her eyes)

Deshawn: Well, you're doing a good job so far.

Stacey: (She begins to sound tired) Why, thank you. D?

Deshawn: Yes?

Stacey: I like where we are.

Deshawn: You mean on the floor?

Stacey: No.

Deshawn: Then where?

Stacey: Us being together. I like it a lot. I love it for lack of a better word.

Deshawn: That's a nice word.

Stacey: Would you say it?

Deshawn: Maybe. (Stacey slowly slides off of his back. Just then, she notices some old cuts on his right wrist)

Stacey: What's this? (Deshawn slowly opens his eyes as he responds)

Deshawn: Reminders I've had enough of. Nothing you should worry about.

Stacey: As long as that's all they are. I don't want to see you hurt. (She lays her arm on his back and falls asleep.

Deshawn: Neither do I. (Deshawn slowly begins to sleep as well)

CHAPTER 13

▼

Deshawn Narrarates: The biggest thing that sucks about guys getting dumped is when the women who do it give you the dumbest or simplest reason to dump you. Simple I can do, but the dumb ones even to this day make no sense to me. Still annoys me a times, but why fight fire with fire if you have a fire extinguisher right? I guess that line makes some sense. At least I think it does, but oh well.

(He begins to have another flashback. This begins when he was eighteen years old. He rides in the passenger seat as another woman drives. She parks in front of a home and cuts off the engine)

Girl: Looks like this is your stop.

Deshawn: Appears so. I'll see you later. (He leans to her to give her a hug. As he reaches for the door handle, she stops him)

Girl: Wait, before you go I have to tell you something.

Deshawn: What?

Girl: I really hate to say this, but I don't think this would work out.

Deshawn: If you mean me getting a car of my own, I have a few paychecks from the job left.

Girl: Not that. I mean with you and me.

Deshawn: Say what?

Girl: Don't get me wrong, you're a great guy, but I'm just not ready for this kind of relationship yet.

Deshawn: If you weren't ready, then why didn't you have a problem dating me in the first place?

Girl: You were just this sweet guy and I liked you a lot, but since yesterday ... (Deshawn cuts her off)

Deshawn: So let me get this straight, you liked me until I asked you out? (Chuckles) I can not believe this. So what was your plan after? Go for the two-for-one special which consisted of not only dumping me after going out, but in front of my own home too? Was this your well thought out master plan?

Girl: I'm sorry.

Deshawn: You've gone way past that. (He opens the door)

Girl: Wait. We can still be friends.

Deshawn: A piece of advise for you; a friend likes you for who you are. What they don't do is piss back steps out of fear. A friend respects a person like me, you don't. (He slams her car door and walks away. The girl watches him for a moment as her eyes begin to become watery. She looks down and slowly starts the engine and pulls away. Deshawn wakes up from his dream. He tries to open his eyes as he looks over to see that Stacey is still sleeping next to him. He slowly begins to get up. As he crouches on the floor, he looks at her resting peacefully) I can't believe you're doing this. So many choices, but never enough chances. Can you be worth the risk? Let's see where this goes. (He picks her up off the floor and lays her on his bed. He covers her under his blanket and lays down beside her on top of it. He lays with his eyes open for a while and then later closes them. Hours pass, a phone rings in the back round. Deshawn opens his eyes a little and tries to reach the dresser for his phone. He finally finds it and puts it to his ear) Hello? Speaking. (He slowly begins to get up from the bed) You did? What happened? Well, do you know where she is? Can I see her? Can I at least talk to her? (Stacey begins to wake up by over hearing Deshawn voice) Please don't do this, you have no idea how long it took me to find her. I'm the only family that little girl has got left. I can't believe this. Fine, whatever. Thanks for nothing. (He hangs up the phone. Stacey watches Deshawn as he holds his head down facing his computer desk. He holds the monitor tightly and moments later, he lets out a loud scream and begins kicking the desk repeatedly. Stacey jumps back in the bed as she watches his shocking fit of rage. Deshawn begins to get tired and stops. He sits on his desk while breathing heavily. Stacey slowly scoots to the edge of the bed and continues to watch him as he tries to calm down) I'm sorry about that.

Stacey: What happened?

Deshawn: I wish I could tell you, but I can't. It's too personal to me and to the people who really know me.

Stacey: But I want to really know you. You just can't keep bottling up all of this anger without telling someone.

Deshawn: You really want to know?

Stacey: Yes, I do.

Deshawn: Okay. (He gets up and walks slowly to her. He opens the dresser drawer next to her and takes out a photograph and hands it to her) She's why. (Stacey looks at the picture. It's of a little girl)

Stacey: Oh my god. She's beautiful. Who is she?

Deshawn: Her name is Renee. That's my little girl.

Stacey: This is your daughter?

Deshawn: No, but she always was to me though. She turns eight this year.

Stacey: Who is she then? (Deshawn walks to his computer desk and sits on top of it)

Deshawn: She's my niece. I practically raised her since she was first born since her real father didn't. Her mother is my older sister, but she never was real good at parenting either. You know, in the three years I've been with that little girl, I have never missed an important moment in her life from her first words to her very first steps. I can still remember that she was so stuck on me, that every day she would try to find me in the house to either play with her or when she needed someone to hold her when she was crying. I also remember whenever her mother would come to get her, Renee would cry at the drop of a hat and try to force herself from not leaving my side. Anyway, years later, my sis (He cuts himself off as his eyes begin to water. He holds them back as he stops for a moment) her mother grew more hatred towards my father and my step-mom. Then in her form of idiotic rebellion, she took her away from me and never looked back. I never saw her again since. After everything that I've been through, that little girl was the only thing that kept giving me the reason to keep living and when she left, that reason left with her.

Stacey: What happened after that?

Deshawn: Well, I found out that her mom went crazy and got thrown in jail and Renee had to go to a foster home. I've been using the past few years trying to find her.

Stacey: That's what the envelope and the call was about?

Deshawn: Yep and in even worse news, the call was from the court office in the state she's in. Apparently, she's with another family happy and healthy, but without me to witness it.

Stacey: What did your dad say?

Deshawn: He told me that I should let her go. That she would be different if I saw her again. She wouldn't remember me. I can't do that. For three years, she was the light I never thought I would ever see and now I'm told that I have to forget and move on. Let me tell you something, there is no forgetting and there is definitely no moving on. (Stacey gets up from the bed and walks to him. She places her hand on his shoulder) Renee was more than just a child, she was my child. And now she's gone. That's like taking your own heart away from you, the only thing that makes you feel anything and keeps you alive. She made me feel again. How can you let go of something like that?

Stacey: Come here. (She hugs him) I'm sorry you had to go through that. I must've been hard.

Deshawn: It's cool. It happens right?

Stacey: Not to people who don't deserve it. (Deshawn sighs) Are you going to be okay?

Deshawn: (She lets go) Yeah. (Seconds later, he turns his head to the side with his eyes shut tight)

Stacey: What's wrong?

Deshawn: I think someone's calling you.

Stacey: What makes you say that?

Deshawn: Because your phone's vibrating my butt.

Stacey: Oh, I'm so sorry.

Deshawn: It's okay. (She reaches behind him and grabs her phone. At the last second she catches a glance at the name. It was Becky) So who'd you miss?

Stacey: It was restricted.

Deshawn: Bill collectors?

Stacey: No way.

Deshawn: Good, if there's one thing I know, is that if you owe to anybody, your phone will never stop ringing. (Her phone rings again. Deshawn looks to Stacey) All right now that's just weird.

Stacey: Hold on. (She takes a few steps back and answers the phone) Hello? (It's Becky on the other line)

Becky: What are you doing?

Stacey: Hi. What's up?

Becky: (She talks to her as she flips through a magazine) Are you doing something that you are not supposed to?

Stacey: Of course not.

Becky: Good! Listen, we need to go out shopping again. I just found this dress that I just have to have and I need a special someone to help with an opinion. How soon can you be ready?

Stacey: Can I call you back in a couple of minutes?

Becky: Sure, but hurry up. I've got a feeling that it will be quite an exciting day for us.

Stacey: All right then. I'll talk to you later. Bye.

Becky: Bye. (She hangs up the phone) You should get ready too. (She looks to her side. Marcus sits in a chair as he reads a history book) You have got quite a day ahead of you. (Marcus is unresponsive) Mark. (He looks to her)

Marcus: Say what?

Becky: You should wait outside now. Remember to wait for my call.

Marcus: (He shrugs his shoulders and sighs as he get up) If you say so. I got one question though, what makes you think this girl wants me in the first place?

Becky: Trust me, after you left, she couldn't stop talking about you.

Marcus: What about her and D?

Becky: Just friends. She's got a boyfriend out of state.

Marcus: That's not what I heard.

Becky: (She gets out of bed and walks to him. She begins to adjust his clothes) Why is it that people only hear things from other people and never listen to source that spoke it? Probably another one of those centuries old questions that no one talks about. Look if you don't want to do this then just say it.

Marcus: If what you say is true, then I'm down.

Becky: Good, finally Miss Stacey can catch herself a good man instead of a no good trash talker like D? You wouldn't believe the things he says about me and all I ever wanted to do was be his friend.

Marcus: What does he say? (Becky looks at him unresponsive. Back in Deshawn's room, Stacey begins to get dressed)

Deshawn: So who was that?

Stacey: What?

Deshawn: On the phone.

Stacey: Oh, sorry. That was my mom. She wanted to see how I was doing.

Deshawn: She wanted to see how you were doing so much that you have to leave?

Stacey: No, it's just that I just remembered some shopping that I had to get done.

Deshawn: That's cool.

Stacey: What were you about to do?

Deshawn: Probably go to the gym and work out for a little bit. Jose should be here in a minute. (At that moment, Jose bursts through the door and slams it shut. He leans on the door soaking wet as he breathes hard) Speak of the devil. What's wrong with you?

Jose: Dog, there is this wild water fight going on in the hallway. I damn near drowned trying to get here. (He cracks open the door and a water balloon explodes on the ground by the door. Jose quickly closes the door for a moment and opens it back) You're going to have to try harder than that bitches! (Another water balloon flies toward the door and Jose closes it again) You ready D?

Deshawn: (He begins to put on a sweat suit on) Way ahead of you. We're heading to the gym right?

Jose: Of course. I grow tired of seeing those toothpicks you call arms. (He spots Stacey) Hi. Didn't know you had company. Stuff like this is normal on the weekends.

Stacey: I'm beginning to notice that more.

Deshawn: Good deal. Get your stuff. I got the door.

Jose: Bet. (He goes to his clothes drawer and gets some gym clothes)

Deshawn: (He looks to Stacey) You ready?

Stacey: For what?

Deshawn: To go back to your place.

Stacey: Is it even safe out there?

Deshawn: Don't worry, I'll protect you.

Stacey: (She puts on her jacket) Okay.

Deshawn: Jose?

Jose: Ready.

Deshawn: All right. Get ready to book. (He walks to the door. He opens it a crack to look outside to see that down the hallway there is a huge water fight going. Deshawn opens the door the rest of the way and the group sneaks out. One of the kids at the end of the hallway spots D and the others walking)

Teen: There's D! (The other teens see them as well and begin running armed with water balloons and squirt guns)

Deshawn: Start running! (The three begin running down the hallway to the stairs. The teens begin shooting water at them, but Deshawn and the others escape to safety outside the dorm. Moments later, the three make it to Stacey's dorm) See, what did I tell you? Safe and fully dry.

Stacey: That was fun. I should probably go.

Deshawn: I'll talk to you later then.

Stacey: Okay. (The two share another moment)

Deshawn: (He looks to Jose) Let's roll.

Stacey: Wait.

Deshawn: Yeah?

Stacey: (She quickly walks to him to kiss him goodbye) Have fun.

Deshawn: Thank you. I will.

Stacey: (She begins to walk backwards away from Deshawn) Be careful.

Deshawn: Always. (She turns and walks away)

Jose: Man you have got to tell me what is the deal with you two. (The two turn around and begin walking)

Deshawn: I will later.

Jose: By the time that later comes around, you would've forgotten.

Deshawn: No I won't. (As the two talk Marcus watches them from a stone bench outside as his friends sit around him. One of the teens speaks to him. It's Matt, Becky's boyfriend)

Matt: There he is. You ready Mark?

Marcus: Let's do this. (Inside the gym, Deshawn is lifting weights on one of the machines as Jose watches him)

Jose: So, when are you talking?

Deshawn: About Stacey?

Jose: Who do you think?

Deshawn: There's not much to say actually. She's cool people.

Jose: Really. She hasn't been trying to hide anything from you or nothing?

Deshawn: Don't get me wrong, there have been times where I have been at least a little suspicious of her actions, but they turn out to be nothing though.

Jose: You sure?

Deshawn: Yeah.

Jose: Just checking.

Deshawn: Why?

Jose: No reason.

Deshawn: Why would you ask me about her as if you knew something?

Jose: What are you talking about?

Deshawn: I'm just checking to see if there is something that you need to tell me that's all.

Jose: Of course not, if there was I would've told you already.

Deshawn: Just checking.

Jose: So, everything is cool with you two right?

Deshawn: I don't know. Ever since I noticed that Becky knew her, I have had my share of doubts.

Jose: Example.

Deshawn: Like today. Everything was fine up until her phone rang and then all of a sudden, she forgets to go shopping. I don't know.

Jose: You think something's up?

Deshawn: There are possibilities.

Jose: What if they are bad ones? (Deshawn doesn't respond) D?

Deshawn: Your turn. (He gets up from the weight machine)

Jose: That was the last set. I got to make a call real quick. (He runs to his gym bag and looks for his phone. He searches for a number and dials. He puts the phone to his ear) Kevin. What's up, it's Jose. Hey, did you find out anything yet?

Kevin: (He sits outside with Quinn) Maybe, I just overheard some stuff about Stacey.

Jose: Like what?

Kevin: You know Marcus right?

Jose: Yeah, the school pimp.

Kevin: Well, he was looking for D earlier today. Some stuff about him talking crap about Becky and what not.

Jose: When was this?

Kevin. Not to long ago.

Jose: Where's Mark?

Kevin: He ran off somewhere. I don't know where though.

Jose: Where are you?

Kevin: I'm with Quinn and Erika outside the gym.

Jose: I'll be there in a second.

Kevin: All right peace.

Jose: (He runs to Deshawn) Hey D, I got to find Quinn and Kevin real quick. I'll be right back cool?

Deshawn: All right. I'm going to get my stuff on.

Jose: Cool. Meet me at the locker room all right?

Deshawn: Cool.

Jose: I'll be just a second. (He runs out of the gym. As he runs toward Kevin, he spots Becky walking up to Stacey outside of her dorm. He looks back to Kevin)

Kevin: Was you running all the way up here?

Jose: No, I walked first and then in an act of sheer happiness, I wanted to run. What do you think?

Kevin: I think that. (He points to Becky walking with Stacey walking towards the gym) Did you notice that too?

Jose: Yeah, I did. I thought she had some shopping to do?

Quinn: I guess not.

Jose: I was hoping to catch Mark to see what was going on. Do you know where he went?

Kevin: He said he was going to the gym to work out.

Jose: What!? Why didn't you say that before?

Kevin: I just found out now.

Jose: D's still in the locker room. (Erika's eyes widen and she quickly runs to the gym)

Quinn: Son of a bitch! (They all run behind Erika)

CHAPTER 14

▼

Deshawn Narrarates: Now one of the most irritating issues that I have is from people wanting to pick a fight with me. One on one I can handle. Groups, not so much. Besides, what all else can a person say who's about to get jumped by a handful of people?

(Deshawn finishes putting on his clothes in the locker room. Marcus and Matt walk up from behind him. Deshawn leans forward to get out of their way. Before he can, Marcus quickly grabs him and throws him into the locker behind him)

Marcus: 'Sup little bitch. I heard you were talking mess about some people I know.

Matt: Yeah. What you got to say now, you punk ass little bastard! (He punches Deshawn in his stomach and picks him back up)

Marcus: Hold up, I got this. (He punches Deshawn in the face and throws him back onto the locker) Why aren't you talking now? (He lands another blow to Deshawn's jaw. Deshawn falls to the ground and struggles to get back up)

Matt: What happened to you being the only one standing? (He kicks him while he is down. Deshawn gathers what's left of his strength to punch Matt in the groin and then in his face. Marcus and another jock begin assaulting Deshawn. Jose and the others run as fast as they can into the locker room. Marcus knees Deshawn in the stomach and punches him again in the face. As Deshawn staggers nearly broken, Marcus throws him into an open locker and slams it shut. The group begins to kick the locker repeatedly. Jose steps onto a bench and jumps into the air and lands on top of Matt and begins punching him. Kevin, Quinn and Erika come up from behind and assault the remaining three. Erika pushes one of the jocks against a locker, but before she can hit him, the teen backhands Erika in the face. Erika holds her face)

Erika: Bad move. (She kicks him in the leg and begins landing blow after blow. Kevin stands up and looks to Jose and tries to pull him off of Matt, but Jose is extremely persistent to keep fighting. Kevin finally manages to get Jose to stop. Jose looks to the locker as he tries to calm his breathing. He slowly opens the locker and Deshawn falls out bleeding nearly from everywhere unconscious. Before hitting the ground, Erika and Jose catch him and try to hold him up)

Jose: Kevin call the hospital. (Kevin pulls his phone from his pocket and begins to dial. Quinn and Jose hold up Deshawn and carry him out of the gym. Erika looks to everyone else watching him. As they walk, Erika notices Stacey and Becky at the top of the stairs looking to see who she is carrying. They slowly make it up the stairs and outside. Jose opens the door to Deshawn's room and lay him down on his bed. Erika races to the bathroom to find medical supplies needed to help stop his bleeding)

Jose: I can't believe this.

Kevin: Neither can I.

Jose: What would make them do something like this? (Erika walks out of the bathroom with some gauze and sits next to Deshawn)

Erika: I might know who.

Quinn: Becky?

Erika: Who else?

Quinn: That's kind of far fetched don't you think? I mean the girl is capable of a lot of things, but doing what I think you think she's doing? I just don't understand that.

Erika: What's there to understand? Our best friend was nearly killed and I put my life that that sleaze knows why. That's probably the reason why they were watching us when we were leaving.

Jose: I'm with Erika on this. I mean we saw them walking to the gym almost right before D got beat up. There's got to be an explanation for all of this.

Erika: I for sure don't want one. I want payback. (Someone knocks on the door. Erika quickly stands up and walks to it, but Jose stops her)

Jose: Help him first. (Erika steps back and goes back to helping Deshawn. Jose opens the door and Stacey walks in)

Stacey: Where's D? (She sees Deshawn on the bed and drops her bag. She puts her hand to her face and begins to cry. Erika stands up and backs away from her clenching her fists. Stacey kneels to him) What happened?

Jose: He got jumped in the locker room.

Stacey: Oh my god. Who would do this?

Jose: We don't know who.

Erika: The important question is; why were you with Becky when it happened?

Stacey: We were about to go shopping.

Erika: So, you decided to check out the gym when you got done?

Stacey: (She looks to Erika) You think I had something to do with this?

Erika: I just think that it's pretty odd that before shopping, you were going to see who was at the gym.

Stacey: Becky wanted to see a friend.

Erika: Who?

Stacey: I don't know who. Why are you asking me all of these questions at a time like this?

Erika: Because I want answers. You were doing pretty well at keeping the promise that I asked you to keep. It's too bad that I'm getting my doubts now.

Stacey: I would never do anything to hurt D and you know that. I kept my promise to him.

Erika: I wasn't talking about that promise. I meant the one you made to me. Since you didn't keep you end, (She begins to crack her knuckles) I get to keep mine. (Before she can walk up to Stacey, Jose stops her. Stacey jumps back)

Jose: Erika stop! Back off!

Erika: Look at him! Look at what happened to D. Something is wrong here and ever since he met her a lot of fishy things have been going on. You know that getting me in a pissed off mood is a bad idea and this broad has got me at my breaking point.

Jose: Don't you think I know that? Just tone it down. Getting pissed isn't helping anything.

Erika: But it makes me feel better.

Stacey: I don't believe this. All I wanted to do was care for him. I would never do anything to hurt him.

Erika: Well, he looks pretty hurt now don't you think?

Jose: Quiet! (He looks to Stacey) Look, right now, I think that it would be a pretty good idea for you to leave now. (Stacey walks to the door. Quinn tries to stop her, but she quickly throws her hand away and walks out the door. Moments later after a silence from the group, someone knocks on the door again. Erika reaches for the door, again Jose stops her) Erika! (He opens the door. It's the paramedics. They look over Deshawn and get him ready to be placed onto a flatbed. The paramedics take Deshawn away. As the door closes and Erika watches, she starts to cry. She puts her head on Jose's shoulder. In Stacey's room, she cries on her pillow. Someone knocks softly on her door)

Stacey: Go away! (The person knocks again) Leave me alone! (The door opens and Marcus walks in wearing different clothes. He walks up to her bed and sits next to her legs)

Marcus: I saw you running and I wanted to make sure you were all right.

Stacey: I'm fine. I just want to be alone right now.

Marcus: Well, what's wrong?

Stacey: Were you at the gym today?

Marcus: Yeah why?

Stacey: So you knew about the fight there right?

Marcus: I saw a little.

Stacey: Well, for your information, my boyfriend was beat up there today. So you can see why I'm being anti-social right now.

Marcus: I'm sorry to hear that.

Stacey: It's okay. Now that you know what's wrong, you can leave.

Marcus: Afraid I can't do that. Right now, you are in a moment of crisis and you need someone to help console you. Just so happens that I know someone who can help do that for you.

Stacey: Who?

Marcus: (He reaches in his pocket and pulls out his glasses. He holds out his hand) How are you? My name is Doctor Marcus here to help you out today.

Stacey: (She shakes his hand) Hi. You're pretty young for a doctor.

Marcus: I know. I got a little bit to go before I can actually say that though.

Stacey: That's nice.

Marcus: So let's start. (She shows a grin and they begin to talk and laugh. Time passes)

Stacey: Thanks for making me feel better.

Marcus: No problem. Anytime I can help.

Stacey: Thank you. (She leans to him to give him a hug. She holds him for a moment and sits back)

Marcus: I should probably go.

Stacey: Yeah.

Marcus: I'll talk to you later though. Is that cool?

Stacey: Yeah, that's fine.

Marcus: All right. I see you around. (He gets up and walks to the door) By the way, just how long might your boyfriend be in the hospital anyway?

Stacey: I don't know, could be a few days.

Marcus: I hope he gets better.

Stacey: I hope so too.

Marcus: I'll talk to you tomorrow. Better yet here. (He pulls out a pen and a piece of paper and writes on it) Call me if you have some free time and we'll talk more.

Stacey: All right.

Marcus: You take it easy. It's sad to see a beautiful woman like yourself so sad.

Stacey: You too. Thanks.

Marcus: Bye. (He walks out of the door and heads down the hallway. Becky walks up from behind him)

Becky: So how'd it go?

Marcus: It went well. She's got a lot of love for her man though. Who is he anyway?

Becky: Just some guy she met. Not important.

Marcus: I just can't believe that fool D though. Why would he say those things about you anyway?

Becky: Who knows? The important thing is that he was finally put in his place. Thank you very much.

Marcus: Don't mention it. So what's next?

Becky: Next, there is nothing.

Marcus: Hold up. What do you mean nothing?

Becky: Just as I said. You wanted to know about the girl I'm hooking you up with, so what's the problem?

Marcus: Nothing, it's just that something seems kind of off about all of this.

Becky: You don't trust me now?

Marcus: It's not that, of course I do. I just don't fully understand why all of these things just suddenly pop up out of nowhere. I mean D's cool people and I just can't figure out why he would do what you said he did. Then on top of that tell me that some girl you just met would like a taste of my nuts.

Becky: Let me get this straight; you just beat the living hell out of him and now you question your judgment about it?

Marcus: Yes, I do. After the way Stacey was explaining about what happened to her man, he almost sounds like D, but I thought you said her man was some cat out of state though?

Becky: Look, let's not worry about that now. First, let's just relax and sleep it off. What's done is done.

Marcus: You wouldn't lie to me would you?

Becky: Of course not. Why would I?

Marcus: Let's just say that I hear things too.

Becky: What's that supposed to mean?

Marcus: Forget it.

Becky: No, (She stops him) what do you mean by that?

Marcus: Look, I just said that it's nothing. Can I go now please?

Becky: You think I set this up? Is that it? All I wanted to do was help out a friend and this is the thanks I get? You know what, forget it. If you don't want me help or friendship, then fine. Bye. (She walks away. Marcus thinks for a moment and runs to stop her)

Marcus: Hold on. I'm sorry all right? I was a little out of line.

Becky: Only a little?

Marcus: I won't do it again. I just heard some things from Stacey that seemed kind of odd and it raised a lot of questions. I'm sorry.

Becky: I forgive you. Just don't let it happen again. I don't feel comfortable with myself feeling that the people that I think are my friends think so badly of me.

Marcus: I can understand that. It won't happen again.

Becky: Please see that it won't. We're still friends right?

Marcus: Of course we are.

Becky: Thank you. You really are a great guy you know that?

Marcus: That's what I'm told.

Becky: Stuff like that should happen more often. So now can we finish where we left off at with the whole going to sleep thing?

Marcus: Yeah, sure.

Becky: Thank you. So everything is cool now right?

Marcus: Yeah.

CHAPTER 15

▼

Deshawn Narrarates: Me in a hospital is usually a bad combination. Here I have an excuse. I just got my ass handed to me, gift wrapped like a Christmas present so what else would you expect? The good thing is that I may have overheard my dad talking to my friends not to long ago. It might have been my imagination or it might have been real. The only thing that's important is that I heard my family's voices. Maybe I have more going for me after all.

(At the hospital where Deshawn is staying, his friends sit around him in his room. Deshawn is sitting up in the bed as Jose and Quinn talk to him. Erika stands in the back and watches)

Jose: You been doing okay?

Deshawn: I've been better.

Quinn: Those bruises healed up pretty quick though.

Deshawn: What can I say? I heal fast.

Jose: I see that. (He lightly hits him on the arm and Deshawn quickly yells in pain)

Deshawn: I meant externally. The insides are still hurting like a S.O.B.

Jose: Sorry about that.

Deshawn: Hey, don't even sweat it. (He looks to Erika) Hey, quit looking like the world just ended and give me a hug please.

Erika: Sorry. (She slowly walks up to him. She lightly sniffles)

Deshawn: Why does it sound like you're crying?

Erika: Because I am.

Deshawn: No more of that. I'm fine. (Erika lets go and stands back)

Erika: I know. (She wipes her eyes) It sure doesn't look like it though.

Deshawn: You noticed that too I see?

Quinn: We got to tell you something. We may think that Stacey … (Jose cuts him off)

Jose: We may think that Stacey may be a little late getting here to see you.

Deshawn: I'm not worried about that right now. (Stacey slowly walks up to the door and listens) I just want to know what the hell happened. Why would those fools just jump me like that? On top of that talk all of this stuff about me talking crap about one of their friends just for no reason.

Jose: That we don't know.

Erika: Like hell we don't. (Stacey quickly leaves to hide)

Deshawn: What's wrong Erika?

Erika: Nothing. We should let you get some rest. Come on guys.

Quinn: Take it easy bro.

Deshawn: Please, as long as I have this big-ass needle in my hand and the weird guy I got to share the room with, I won't be.

Quinn: (He laughs) All right short stack. You be easy.

Jose: Later bro.

Deshawn: You all be safe.

Erika: (She walks up to him) Are you going to be okay?

Deshawn: I'm not dead right?

Erika: No.

Deshawn: Then I'll be fine.

Erika: Please don't use that word at a time like this.

Deshawn: What, fine?

Erika: You know what I meant.

Deshawn: Look, Erika I will be okay.

Erika: I know. It's just that I can't lose you.

Deshawn: You're not going to.

Erika: But what if I do? God, you're like the only thing that I've got that's the closest to being someone I (She stops as she starts to cry again)

Deshawn: The closest to what?

Erika: Forget it. (She tries to walk away, but Deshawn grabs her wrist)

Deshawn: Wait. Is there something that you need to tell me?

Erika: I'm sorry. I can't.

Deshawn: Why?

Erika: Because on the day you promised me, I made one too.

Deshawn: What was it?

Erika: I wish I could tell you, but I'm too scared to. Not now.

Deshawn: In all the years we've known each other, I've never seen you this scared before. Why won't you tell me?

Erika: Let's just drop it okay?

Deshawn: Not until you tell me. (She walks up to him and leans in to softly kiss him on his forehead)

Erika: I'll call you tomorrow. (She walks out of the room. Deshawn lays back down in the bed. Moments later, Stacey slowly walks in)

Stacey: I was hoping to make it before visiting hours are over.

Deshawn: (He looks to her) If this place had clocks that worked, I could tell you.

Stacey: How have you been?

Deshawn: Good I guess.

Stacey: May I come in?

Deshawn: What's stopping you?

Stacey: Nothing. (She walks towards a nearby chair and pulls it closer to him. She sits down) I wanted to see you.

Deshawn: I'm here. I'm alive, just barley and almost well.

Stacey: I'm sorry.

Deshawn: Don't be.

Stacey: I've been doing a lot of thinking and I wanted to tell you something.

Deshawn: What's on your mind?

Stacey: Ever since I met you, I have been feeling something that I couldn't explain until now. It's been racing through my head almost all the time, but now I think I understand what's going on.

Deshawn: What is it?

Stacey: D, there has been something that I've been wanting to tell you, but I'm afraid of where it might lead to.

Deshawn: What are you saying?

Stacey: D, I think I'm beginning to fall in love with you.

Deshawn: (He leans his head back a little) That's a little odd don't you think? I mean, you wait until I get beat down to tell me this.

Stacey: I know and I'm sorry, but I had to tell you now. I wanted you to know.

Deshawn: I don't know what to say. You already know why me and that word don't mix all that well.

Stacey: I know, but I wanted you to know what I feel. Can you at least tell me that you have something close to that for me?

Deshawn: I do, to an extent.

Stacey: Thank you. So what happens now?

Deshawn: I don't know. We both know how we feel about each other. What else is there to say?

Stacey: I know. I don't want this to change anything about us.

Deshawn: It won't.

Stacey: Thank you. (She kisses him on the lips and sits back down. She places her head gently on his arm) How much longer do you have to be here?

Deshawn: Probably for a few more days. I'm trying to tell these doctors that I'm fine so I can get the hell out of here. Every time I do, they tell me I have another blood check to do. Any more and I'll need another needle in me to get all my blood back. That and the food tastes like a rancid baboon's booty crack. (Stacey laughs)

Stacey: Aw, does my little baby need some food to eat?

Deshawn: Please, yes. I don't know how much more of this pain I can take. I do like the little juice packs though.

Stacey: Well it's a good thing I brought this. (She reaches down and places a bag on his chest)

Deshawn: You are above a being queen right now.

Stacey: I know. (She leans in to kiss him again) I didn't know what you were in the mood for, so I just got us a burger and fries.

Deshawn: After having to eat what I did, this says a lot.

Stacey: Glad you appreciate it.

Deshawn: That I do. Once again, thank you.

Stacey: Don't mention it. You don't have to say it now. You can when you're ready.

Deshawn: Say what?

Stacey: That word.

Deshawn: Oh, that. Like I said, I want to say it, but I have to make sure that I mean it first. Just like I said, I want to make sure that I'm not going to be wasting it again. I need to know for sure before I even consider saying it.

Stacey: I want you to. I'll be here for you whenever you need me to.

Deshawn: Like now?

Stacey: Before now.

Deshawn: That's good. (She kisses his hand) You got plans for tonight?

Stacey: Just staying here with you was all that I wanted to do today.

Deshawn: That's nice. Visiting hours are going to be up soon.

Stacey: I don't care. The only way I'm leaving is when I get up in the morning.

Deshawn: What about angry nurses?

Stacey: They'll have to put up quite a fight in order to get me out of here.

Deshawn: I'll be there to cheer you on if they try to.

Stacey: That's good. (She sits back in her chair and falls asleep) Good night.

Deshawn: Good night. (He stops to think for a minute. He looks around the room and then to her) Stacey?

Stacey: Yeah?

Deshawn: I (He starts to stutter) Lo … (He stops. Stacey opens her eyes as she starts to piece together what he is trying to say) Stacey, I (He struggles more. Tears begin to form from her eyes) I (He sighs) You know what I mean. (She starts to cry. She quickly leans in to give him a kiss)

Stacey: Thank you.

Deshawn: No, thank you. That took a lot for me to say.

Stacey: That's okay. You did great.

Deshawn: Thanks.

Stacey: (She wipes the tears from her eyes) You should get some sleep.

Deshawn: Yeah. Good night. (She holds his hand) You still want to stay?

Stacey: Nothing makes me feel better than being here with you or anywhere for that matter.

Deshawn: That's cool. (She kisses him again) Now we can sleep. Remind me when I get out of here, that I have something to show you.

Stacey: It's a promise. (She caresses his forehead and goes back to sleep in her chair)

CHAPTER 16

▼

Deshawn Narrarates: The main thing I despise about hospitals is that most of them are quick to pick you up, but even quicker to kick you out. Luckily that didn't happen in this situation. Welcome back to the outside world.

(A few days pass. Jose opens his room door and Deshawn walks inside. Jose follows behind him)

Deshawn: Home sweet home.

Jose: Yeah it is. How do you feel?

Deshawn: Like a slave finally finding freedom.

Jose: I guess that means the word better. (He walks to his desk and tosses a book bag at Deshawn. Deshawn catches it) Here, time to go back to work slave.

Deshawn: What's this?

Jose: Missed homework.

Deshawn: Great. (His phone rings. He sees it ringing on his desk) Could you toss me that please?

Jose: Yeah. (He grabs Deshawn's phone and tosses it to him. Deshawn catches it) Thanks. (He answers) Hello. (It's Stacey on the other line)

Stacey: How are you doing?

Deshawn: Better. Much better, I finally got out and I feel good.

Stacey: That's nice. I didn't forget about what you wanted to show me.

Deshawn: What I wanted to show you? Oh yeah. Sorry about that I just remembered.

Jose: Who's that?

Deshawn: (He covers his phone) Stacey.

Jose: You gonna let her know about the welcome back party we planned for you.

Deshawn: When is it?

Jose: Tonight. So don't get to comfortable.

Deshawn: Well then, when are we going?

Jose: A couple hours from now.

Deshawn: Are you serious? I just got out of the hospital!

Jose: And? People wanted to see you as soon as you got out, so what's the problem?

Deshawn: (He shrugs his shoulders and grins) Okay. (He gets back on the phone with Stacey) Sorry about the long hold.

Stacey: It's okay. When can I see you?

Deshawn: As soon as you want to. Apparently there's a party being held in my honor and I have to get ready for it in a few hours.

Stacey: I'll be there in a few minutes.

Deshawn: Fine with me.

Stacey: Okay I'll se you soon, and D? I love you.

Deshawn: You too. Bye. (He hangs up the phone)

Jose: You never told us you started using that word again.

Deshawn: Last minute conversation I had with her.

Jose: You really mean it this time?

Deshawn: Yeah. I finally think that I'm at that point again.

Jose: Just be careful.

Deshawn: I will. (Time passes and it is dark outside. The moon shines brightly onto a rooftop. Voices are heard behind the door leading to the roof)

Stacey: Where are we going?

Deshawn: I told you, it's a surprise. I can't just tell you what it is though.

Stacey: All right, I trust you.

Deshawn: That's all that matters. (He opens the door while holding her eyes. He guides her to the middle and stops) All right. (He takes away his hand and Stacey looks around)

Stacey: Where are we?

Deshawn: The top of the library. It's where I always go when I want to clear my head.

Stacey: Your friends know about this place too.

Deshawn: They should. They're the ones who helped me find this place.

Stacey: How did you find it?

Deshawn: I got caught in one of my cut parties again and they confronted me about it. I was so pissed off that I ran into the door leading up here. When they caught up with me, everything seemed better between us. I looked around and felt uplifted to say the least. Once they saw that, they figured that this be the place I go to whenever I get those feelings again.

Stacey: They really do have a lot of love for you don't they?

Deshawn: Yeah. If anything ever happens, they always know where to find me. This is the only place where I can clear my head and just forget almost every-thing.

Stacey: Not the important things, I hope.

Deshawn: Never those. Just all the bad things. I try to take the time to deprogram all that stuff from my mind.

Stacey: I like what it's done to you.

Deshawn: Thanks. (His phone rings. He takes his phone from his pocket and answers it) Hello? 'Sup Jose. Cool, we'll be there in a little bit. All right, one. (He hangs up the phone) That's our cue.

Stacey: For what?

Deshawn: My friends are holding a welcome back party for me.

Stacey: Well then, we should get moving.

Deshawn: Let's go. (They leave the library roof and walk towards Kevin's home where the party is being held. The two walk inside. Stacey spots Becky sitting in a corner)

Stacey: (She taps Deshawn on the arm) I'll be right back.

Deshawn: All right. (She walks away. Jose and Erika walk up to him)

Jose: After suffering a major beating, you still walk. I'm beginning to think that you're almost invincible.

Deshawn: Not even death itself can touch me.

Erika: Too true.

Jose: Who'd you come here with?

Deshawn: Stacey.

Erika: (She narrows her eyes a bit) Really? Any idea where she might be?

Deshawn: She stepped out for a minute. She should be around. (Stacey continues to walk to Becky. She doesn't notice that Marcus beside her. Marcus watches her pass and walks up to stop her)

Marcus: (He taps her on the shoulder) Excuse me, miss? (Stacey turns around)

Stacey: Marcus! Hi! (She hugs him) How have you been?

Marcus: I've been good. How about you?

Stacey: I've been doing very well, thank you.

Marcus: So, what are you doing here?

Stacey: It's my boyfriends' welcome back party.

Marcus: (In slight confusion) Your boyfriend?

Stacey: What's wrong?

Marcus: D's your boyfriend?

Stacey: Of course. Why?

Marcus: (He looks around in thought) Nothing. (He looks back to Stacey) I hope he gets better.

Stacey: I hope he does too.

Marcus: Well look, I'm going to get a drink and if you would like to talk, just come find me all right?

Stacey: Sure. (She watches him walk away. She heads towards D. Before she can reach him, she sees Erika standing next to him laughing. She watches for a moment and walks towards him. She taps him on the shoulder) Hi!

Deshawn: Why hello there! Are you having fun yet?

Stacey: Of course I am. (She looks to Erika) Hi.

Erika: (She looks at Stacey with a serious look on her face) Hi.

Stacey: Look, I just wanted to say that I'm (Before she can finish her sentence, Erika cuts her off)

Erika: Save it before I call you out your name.

Stacey: All right then. (She looks back to Deshawn) Would you like to dance for a while?

Deshawn: (He looks to Erika and Stacey for a moment) Sure I will. (He looks to his friends) We'll be back. (The two begin to walk away)

Erika: D! (Deshawn turns around. She looks to him and Stacey together for a moment) Have fun.

Deshawn: We will. (Deshawn and Stacey walk to the middle of the room and dance for a while. Erika watches with a tight fist)

Jose: Keep it cool.

Erika: I am! I just really don't like her right now. (She watches as the two kiss while the song plays) I can't take this. (She walks off)

Jose: Erika wait! (He follows her. Deshawn and Stacey walk back to where his friends' were, but sees that they are nowhere to be found)

Deshawn: Where'd they go?

Stacey: Don't know.

Deshawn: I'll be right back.

Stacey: Be quick.

Deshawn: I will. (He walks away. He heads to the kitchen where he finds Erika and Jose) There you are! I thought you guys went ghost on me for a second.

Jose: We just got cramped up from all the people.

Deshawn: I can understand that.

Erika: So how's your girl?

Deshawn: She's good, thanks.

Erika: All right. (While the group continues to talk, Marcus walks up from behind Stacey and hands her a drink. He signals for her to follow him and wraps his arm around her as the two walk away)

Deshawn: So what's the deal? Ever since I was in the hospital, I've felt like there's this static between us now. What's going on?

Erika: I told you already, it's nothing. So drop it. (She walks past him. Deshawn tries to think about what's going. Before he can, Erika grabs his arm)

Deshawn: What the hell?

Jose: (He yells to them) You kids have a good time out there all right? (Erika leads him through the swarm of people. She stops at on open spot)

Deshawn: What's the matter with you?

Erika: I feel like dancing. (As the two are dancing, they continue to talk)

Deshawn: All right fine. So what's the deal with you anyway? Why the hell have you been so mad at me lately?

Erika: Why are you worrying about that so much?

Deshawn: I have to!

Erika: Why?

Deshawn: Because I care too much for you! Is that hard for you to understand?

Erika: How you feel for me, is not even close to how much I feel for you.

Deshawn: What?

Erika: I said (She sees Stacey talking to Marcus in the corner of the room laughing. She gets angry. She grabs Deshawn's arm and leads him outside) Let's go!

Deshawn: Will the madness ever cease? (He follows her outside. They walk towards the patio. The two lean against the patio fence) Now will you tell me what's wrong?

Erika: Is being with her what you really want?

Deshawn: Yes, it is.

Erika: You're sure about this?

Deshawn: I am very sure.

Erika: Did you at least decide what ring to give her?

Deshawn: No, but now I'm getting an idea on one of them.

Erika: Cool. I just wanted to make sure.

Deshawn: (He nudges her arm) Is that the only reason?

Erika: Of course it is. Whatever makes you happy, that's all that matters.

Deshawn: Thank you. I have a really good feeling that this is going to be a smart move for me.

Erika: You really think so?

Deshawn: The madness has got to end somewhere.

Erika: That is does. So, what happens if you're wrong about this one?

Deshawn: There's nothing wrong now.

Erika: You really believe that?

Deshawn: Hey, she cares a lot about me. She said so herself. Would there be a reason for to fake all that? (Jose still stands in the kitchen talking to Quinn. He looks around and sees Stacey drinking with Marcus. Only this time, the two are closer than before. Jose watches as he sees Marcus lean in and whisper in her ear and places his hand on her leg)

Jose: What the hell?

Quinn: What?

Jose: Something bad. (He takes a sip of his drink. He quickly sets it down) We got to find D. (The two of them walk out. Meanwhile, Deshawn and Erika continue to talk outside)

Deshawn: I should probably go.

Erika: You just got here.

Deshawn: I know, but I need to get this ring crap out of my head. The stuff keeps giving me a headache every time I think about it.

Erika: Then let's do something to get that out. Let's dance for a little longer.

Deshawn: Sounds like a plan. (They walk back inside. Deshawn stares at her tattoo again as he watches her walk away. Erika stops at the door)

Erika: Are you enjoying the view?

Deshawn: Sorry. Force of habit. It won't happen again.

Erika: Really now? That's too bad. (As she walks inside, she adjusts her top to reveal more of her lower back. She puts her hand on her shoulder and Deshawn holds it to follow her. As the two dance, Stacey walks with Marcus outside without Deshawn and Erika noticing. Stacey stops at the door)

Stacey: Wait, I have to tell D that I'm leaving.

Marcus: Sure.

Stacey: Just wait here.

Marcus: All right. (Stacey turns around to find Deshawn. She later sees him with Erika again. She watches them dance for a moment and turns back around to Marcus)

Stacey: On second thought, I'll call him later.

Marcus: If you say so. We should move to a spot that's a little more quiet. (The two walk out. Jose walks up from behind Deshawn and taps him on the shoulder)

Jose: Can I talk to you for a second?

Deshawn: Yeah. (He holds Erika's hand and the group walk back outside) What's up?

Jose: Where's Stacey?

Deshawn: She should still be inside, why?

Jose: When was the last time you saw her?

Deshawn: When we first got here.

Jose: You seen her Erika?

Erika: I saw something.

Jose: (He looks back to Deshawn) And you haven't seen her since?

Deshawn: No. What's going on?

Jose: Before I called you out here, I saw her leaving.

Deshawn: Are you serious? Why would she just up and leave without telling me?

Erika: From the looks of it, she was to busy to even remember.

Deshawn: Say what?

Erika: Nothing.

Jose: You still got her ring?

Deshawn: Yeah. Why?

Jose: It would be in your best interest to give it back.

Deshawn: Why?

Jose: Just trust me on this. Do the right thing and give it back.

Deshawn: Not until you tell me why.

Jose: Look, I don't know how else to say this, but the girl is playing you.

Deshawn: How the hell do you know that?

Jose: Don't worry about that now. Just give it back and walk away from her. Please just do this as a personal favor to all of us.

Deshawn: Are you at least going to tell me why?

Jose: Can't do that.

Deshawn: What the hell is going on here? Why the hell is everyone so persistent to stop me from being with someone that finally cares about me?

Jose: Because she doesn't. I found that out myself not to long ago.

Erika: (She looks to Jose) You saw it too?

Jose: Yeah I did.

Deshawn: Saw what? (Everyone is unresponsive) What did you see? Erika, what did the two of you see? (She looks away and then to the ground) So nobody knows anything now right? You know what? I don't need this. I'm out. (He walks away. Jose tries to stop him)

Jose: D.

Deshawn: (He quickly pulls his hand away) Don't touch me! (He continues to walk away)

CHAPTER 17

▼

Deshawn Narrarates: This was it. The moment of truth. It's time to decide if this girl is worth it or not. A part of me says that I'm finally ready for the next step. The other part expects the worst. Out of everything that has happened so far, is it finally for the better? Then I remember Erika. She cares a lot for me and doesn't want me to get hurt, but some of the things she's been telling me that it's more than that. I can't think about what would happen if I made the wrong choice. Only one way to find out.

(He opens his room door and turns on a lamp as he goes to his dresser drawer. He pulls out two ring boxes. He opens the two boxes and looks at them) Decision time. Which one do I choose? (He shakes his head) I can't believe I'm doing this. (He takes one of the boxes and walks out of the room. He heads towards Stacey's room. He stops at her door and looks to the ring box and sighs) Okay. (Before he grabs the door knob he overhears voices and moaning from inside the room. He looks in confusion for a moment. He attempts to knock on the door, but stops. He listens again as the noises slowly intensify. He thinks again for a moment. He opens the door and takes a step inside. He looks down to see than the floor is littered with clothes and undergarments. He looks at the trail which leads to Stacey's bed. Much to his surprise, he looks to see that the noises were coming from her and Marcus. Deshawn's body begins to gently shake and twitch. His breathing grows short from the shock and he begins to stumble backwards. Stacey sees Deshawn in the doorway while Marcus turns his head to see what she is looking at)

Stacey: Oh my god. D? (Deshawn holds his head in pain. He falls back in to the wall behind him. Images flash in his mind of him slicing his wrist and his moments with Stacey. The words of his arguments and conversations with his friends speak in the back round. Stacey struggles to push Marcus off of her) Get off of me! D wait, I can explain! (She puts on some clothes as quickly as she can and rushes outside) D, please listen to me. I'm so sorry. I never meant for this to happen. Everything happened so fast, I didn't know what was going on! (Deshawn continues to stumble through the hallway. He pushes Stacey off of him and tries to walk away, but due to his shallow breathing he quickly gets dizzy and drops to his knees. Images continue to appear in his mind. Memories of his mother beating him as a child, to him making numerous suicide attempts and negative words that repeat themselves in his mind so fast that they bring close to the brink of insanity. Stacey kneels next to him and tries to get him to look at her as she begins to cry. D continues to hold his head trying to block out what he was trying so hard to get rid of. The more he tries to concentrate, the faster the images and the words come flooding in) D, please look at me. Deshawn, please stop and look at me. D, I'm so sorry. I love you so much. (Deshawn finally gets his footing and pushes her off of him again and runs off. Stacey leans against the wall as she continues to cry. He bursts through the exit doors and almost falls down the stairs. He stops his fall and starts running. Meanwhile; Jose and Quinn walk through the parking lot. Snow begins to fall)

Jose: Why in the hell does it have to snow now? And why in the hell is it so damn cold! First Erika gets pissed, then D, and now I am straight up livid. God, I hate this state so much sometimes! (Jose notices Deshawn running away from Stacey's dorm) Is that D?

Quinn: Where?

Jose: Right there. (He points to him running) I'll be damned, that is him. D! (Deshawn continues to run. The two head begin to run after him. They run into their dorm thinking that Deshawn ran inside. Jose bursts open their room door and looks around) D! D, are you in here? (He looks to Deshawn's bed and sees one closed ring case) Damn it!

Quinn: You think he gave her that other ring?

Jose: Looks like he was about to. Based on what we saw, it didn't go to well.

Quinn: Well then, where the hell is he?

Jose: Shut up and let me think. Now, if I were D in a very pissed off mood, where would I go?

Quinn: (The idea comes to him) The library!

Jose: Oh hell! (He runs to the window and sees the snow is getting thicker) Damn it! Get some extra clothes. (Quinn digs through dressers for cold weather gear as Jose continues to look outside. He clenches his fist and punches the desk)

Quinn: I got them!

Jose: Let's go. (The two run outside. Later, Deshawn bursts through the door to the roof of the library and struggles to the edge. He begins to take off his sweater and drops to his knees and falls to the ground. He closes his eyes. Moments later, he opens them and tries to stand up. He uses the strength he has left to scream to the sky to say the one thing he has never had the courage to say until now)

Deshawn: I fucking hate you!!! (He drops to his knees and slumps his head down to the frozen ground) I can't do this anymore. (He looks to the sky again and screams) What do you want from me? What did I do to deserve this? (He leans down, closer to the ground with his head in his arms) Was it because I wasn't strong enough? Is it because I was born? If that's the cause, then why was I even born in the first place? I can't do this anymore. (He looks over the edge of the building and looks below. He slowly steps up on the ledge and stops. He looks at the sky again) Is this what you want? Fine. (He looks at the people below) If this is what I have to do, then so be it. (He continues to look as he sees people walking around the area. He closes his eyes tightly and lets out a breath. He slowly leans forward as begins to release his grip. Jose and Quinn struggle to cut through the mild snow shower while on their way to the library. Once there, the two burst through the doors and run towards the ladder leading to the roof. Their snowy shoes echo through the library as they dash inside. As they reach the ladder leading to the roof, the two see how far it is from the ground and that nothing was placed in front of it showing them that Deshawn didn't bother to use anything to help him reach it)

Quinn: Damn that boy has hops when he's pissed.

Jose: Enough with that. Give me a boost. (Quinn kneels down to help Jose reach the ladder. Once Jose gets high enough, Quinn jumps up to grab the last rung of the ladder and proceeds to follow. Deshawn finally lets' go and falls off the ledge. As he falls slowly to the ground below, he begins to remember the good times he shared with his friends and family and how happy they were around him. They continue to appear rapidly, until everything suddenly goes black. There's no sound of impact. Seconds later, Jose makes it to the top and bursts through the roof door. He sees Deshawn's body lay nearly lifeless on the snowy rooftop and shaking hard as it grows too cold for him to take) Oh my god! Quinn, call the ambulance now! (He runs to his body and takes off his coat. He wraps Deshawn in it, picks him up and runs back inside. He lays his body on the ground and tries to keep him warm. Quinn runs up to him) Did you call them?

Quinn: Yeah, they should be here soon. Oh God. Is he going to be okay?

Jose: Don't know yet. I can't get a pulse from him.

Quinn: Well, is there something we can do?

Jose: I don't know yet! Look, right now all we can do is wait.

Quinn: But he can't!

Jose: Don't you think I know that?

Quinn: So then what are we supposed to do then?

Jose: I said I don't know! Let's just try to calm down focus on the problem at hand which is taking care of him until help comes. Can you help me do that please?

Quinn: Why would he do something like this?

Jose: I got a few ideas. (The paramedics run into the library and rush to the group. They swarm around his body as they begin working on him. They all pick Deshawn up and place him onto a flatbed and carry him out while keeping him covered. As they walk out Erika walks as a group of students watch what's going on. She walks up from behind one of the students)

Erika: What's going on?

Student: Don't know. Someone was stuck up on the roof. Almost like they were trying to jump off or something. (Her eyes widen as she watches the medics leave. Time passes. Jose and Quinn watch Deshawn lying in a heated tub while doctors and nurses watch over him checking his vitals)

Jose: I can't believe this is happening.

Doctor: He's going to be all right. It's just a matter of time before he can fully regain his normal body temperature. (As he speaks to them, Erika walks slowly up the stairs and listens to what's being said) I must say it's a good thing that he has such good friends that care about him. If he had been out there for a few more minutes, he might not have made it.

Jose: Thanks doc. (The doctor walks away)

Quinn: What will we tell Erika? (Erika turns her head and continues to listen)

Jose: We aren't telling her jack. If she found out about this, she'll beat the hell out of Becky, damn near kill Stacey and then come after us for not telling her about D. Whatever happens we don't say nothing, all right. Erika can not know about this.

Erika: (She speaks from behind the two) Too late.

Jose: (He looks in shock) Erika! Hi! How long have you been there?

Erika: Long enough. Is that D?

Jose: Where?

Erika: If you give me a stupid answer again, I will beat the hell out of you and have you castrated with a rusted butter knife. Now I'm going to ask you again, is that D?

Jose: (He pauses for a moment. He looks away as he tries to think of the proper way to tell her) Yeah.

Erika: And when did you plan on telling me?

Jose: We were hoping that we wouldn't have to.

Erika: Really? Well that's nice to hear. Excuse me. (She pushes the two aside and walks in the room. She sees Deshawn's near lifeless body in the heated tub with tubes from all over his body. She slowly walks closer as she begins to cry. She then sniffles as she speaks to Jose) Where is she?

Jose: Who?

Erika: Who do you think?

Jose: We don't know.

Erika: (She quickly responds) Where does she live?

Jose: I think that she lives in the dorm across from us, but (Before he finishes his sentence, Erika darts out of the room and down the stairs) Erika wait! (He follows her to the stairwell. He stops at the top as she reaches the middle) Erika! (She stops) Where are you going?

Erika: (She looks to him) Girl talk. (She continues down the stairs)

CHAPTER 18

▼

Deshawn Narrarates: I say this to everyone who knows this girl. Pissing off Erika is absolutely, positively, and ultimatley the worst thing anyone can do. Especially when it comes to me.

(Erika walks inside Stacey's dorm. As she proceeds up the stairs, she sees Becky walking out of her room and going down the hallway. Erika's walking speed quickens. She gets within a few feet behind Becky and taps her on the shoulder)

Erika: Excuse me. (Before Becky can fully turn around to see who it is, Erika lands a hard right cross to Becky's face. Becky quickly falls to the ground. Erika kneels down and rests her head on her arms) Hi. Someone I care about nearly died today. I just wanted to let you know how I felt about that. (Becky struggles to get up, but Erika quickly backhands her back to the floor) Now you get to tell me where Stacey is so I can tell her too. (Becky tries to wipe off the blood from her chin and sit herself up, but Erika grabs her head and shoves it against the nearby wall) I'm not done yet. You have pissed me off for the last time. (She grabs Becky by the hair and pulls back) You don't have the slightest clue as to how important Deshawn is to me. I am so close to going just a bit over the edge with you, but I won't. It's people like you that make someone like Deshawn so important. This will be the last and final time you do this. (She stops for a moment as she looks at Becky) You look pretty bad. I'm so sorry about that. Here, let me help you up. (She grabs Becky by the arm and helps her up. She brushes her off) Do you know where she might be? Stacey I mean. (She sees Marcus watching from his doorway) Hold that thought please. Be right back. (She takes a few steps and stops as she snaps her fingers) Before I forget again. (She slaps her to the ground again with an open palm and walks towards Marcus) I got a good idea that you might know something. You and that little whore Stacey hurt someone very important to me. Now I want to you to tell me where she is. Right now I'm the bitch that you really, really don't want to get more pissed off. So you got two choices, you can either prefer to be stupid about it, or we can get ghetto nuts right here and now.

Marcus: Look, if it's about your friend, I'm sorry. I'm shocked too. Becky was full of lies from the start. I never meant for any of this to happen.

Erika: I didn't ask you that.

Marcus: Look, I said I was sorry! What more do you want?

Erika: You men are all the same, nothing, but dogs. You all act like this is just some game. You don't care who you hurt to win. All that interests you is getting what you want. D was a good man. He is a great man and you nearly destroyed him for what, a piece of ass? Well then, since you were so eager to take him away from me, I'm just gonna take these away from you. (She squeezes harder)

Marcus: So what do you want me to do?

Erika: (She chuckles) Well, for starters. (She quickly grabs his groin and squeezes tightly. Marcus quickly stumbles back in excruciating pain. He tries to pull her hand off, but her grip is too tight for him to do so) Tell her that I want to talk to her now. Not later, but right now. If you don't, I swear to God, I will put you through so much pain you would wish your parents never even considered of having you conceived. I'm trying to be nice to you right now. I mean, it's not everyday that people see me this angry. (She looks down to her hand) That's odd, (She looks back to Marcus) doesn't look like you have much to work with here. So, as a personal favor to me, you tell her, or this noodle that you use as a Frisbee will be in a real dogs mouth. You got that? Can you do that for me please?

Marcus: (His voice is high pitched from the pain as he yells out) Yes!

Erika: You sure? You won't lie to me would you? I really don't like it when people do that.

Marcus: No! No! Please stop! I'll tell her!

Erika: I'm sorry I didn't quite catch that. You said you'll do what? (She tightens her grip and Marcus yells louder)

Marcus: I'll tell her!

Erika: Great thanks. (She lets go and Marcus quickly falls to the floor shivering. She leans down to him) Nice talking to you. You should probably get some ice for that. I hear it hurts like hell. (She walks out of the room. As she leaves, she walks past Becky. Becky quickly presses her back against the wall. Erika stops and walks up to her) I was wrong. I shouldn't have hit you. It's just that after seeing D in that hospital bed, I kind of got a little on edge. It's a bad habit of mine I apologize. (She takes a few steps to walk away, but stops) Then again, I just can't shake the fact that (She quickly backhands her again) I really don't like you. (Erika looks down at Becky and releases a small grin of satisfaction and walks away. Later, she walks up the stairs in the hospital with her arms crossed. Jose quickly gets out of the chair that he is resting in. Quinn sits asleep in his. Jose walks to Erika)

Jose: Are you all right?

Erika: I'm fine. I just need to be alone with him for a while.

Jose: Okay. I'll be outside if you need me.

Erika: Thank you. (She slowly walks inside and looks at Deshawn. She slowly walks closer to him) So, here we are again. You in the hospital just inches away from leaving me again. Why did you want to break the promise you made to me so long ago? I miss what we had and most of all, I miss you. (She sniffles as she places her hand on his head) I miss your energy, your sense of humor, and most of all, your independence. I loved the way you held yourself around people. You were the only one who wasn't afraid to speak the truth about things. We've been through so much together. Over the past few days, I finally realized how much I care about you. I can't lose you again. (She slowly begins to break down) I won't. So, you're going to get better and you're going to make it through this. You're going to come back to me. Please D, don't have me live without you. (She kisses his forehead. As she does, Deshawn's eyes gently twitch. She steps back as she covers her face. She turns to walk away. Before she can reach the door, Deshawn weakly calls to her)

Deshawn: Hey. (She stops. Deshawn looks to her as he tries to clear his throat) You could've just woke me up. (She turns around and runs to him)

Erika: D! Are you okay? How do you feel?

Deshawn: Like a lab rat.

Erika: You nearly froze to death.

Deshawn: Really now? Remind me never to do that again, would you please?

Erika: (Chuckles) It's a promise.

Deshawn: Some party huh?

Erika: Sure was.

Deshawn: Where are the others?

Erika: They're outside.

Deshawn: Did I miss anything?

Erika: There were some things that happened while you were out.

Deshawn: That's nice.

Erika: You should get some sleep. Good night.

Deshawn: Good night. (She turns and walks away) Hey. (She turns around again) You really meant what you said about me? How you would miss me if I was gone?

Erika: Every word. Good night. (She walks out of the room. She stops at the outside of the wall and leans against it. She then thinks for a moment and then breaks out into tears. She slowly sits down curling herself up with her knees close to her chest as she continues to weep. Days pass. The door to Deshawn's room opens and he walks inside with Jose and Quinn)

CHAPTER 19

▼

Deshawn Narrarates: Once again, welcome back to the outside world. It wasn't a frightening experience, but it's one I can't have in my life again. My eyes are fully open and I can finally see what I've been missing. All there is to do now is show the people who put me through this that I'm not easy to put down.

Quinn: Here we are again. Home sweet home.

Deshawn: It sure does feel good to be back. I sure do miss that Jacuzzi bed I was in though.

Jose: Exactly, that's why they were so happy to send you back to ordinary living.

Deshawn: Oh joy. (He looks to a large stack of books and papers on his bed) What the hell's this?

Jose: Your homework bright boy. Better get cracking. (Jose and Quinn start to walk out)

Deshawn: How am I going to get all of this done?

Jose: (He looks in thought) Don't know. (He looks to Deshawn with a smile on his face) See ya'! (He slams the door)

Deshawn: Wonderful. (He grabs a small stack of papers and places them on his desk. The next day in class the Professor stands before his students)

Professor Peters: (He leans on the front end of his desk as he talks to the students) Ladies and gentlemen. I hope you all had a good weekend. I do not know if many of you received the news I did. While grading your papers, I received a phone call from the local hospital and found out that one of my best students fell victim to an attempt at taking his own life. I want you all to understand that life is a very precious thing and is not something to throw away. His name was Deshawn Keith. By far the best, the brightest, and most influential students that have ever entered this school. (The door at the top of the classroom opens and a student walks inside. He proceeds down the stairs as the teacher speaks. Students from the back leading to the front watch in awe as they see who it is) Irregardless of the problems that he had, he is one of the few students refused to accepts the hand he's been dealt countless times over. I hope that all of you will understand that no matter what happens, all of you have a reason for being. You are all individuals no matter what anyone tells you. That is something that everyday he showed us. I have a card being passed around the room. If you all could sign it for him, it would be greatly appreciated. (He walks to the other side of his desk and continues to speak before he sits down) People like him are what's needed in this day and age. He deserves a lot of respect for what he's done. With that in mind (He looks up to see who walks down the steps. It's Deshawn. Becky watches him from her usual seat. Stacey watches from a far corner of the room. Deshawn mildly struggles down the stairs and walks up to the Professor)

Deshawn: I believe this was due today. (He hands him a stack of papers)

Professor Peters: Mr. Keith. What are you doing here?

Deshawn: This was due today right?

Professor Peters: Yes, but (Deshawn cuts him off politely)

Deshawn: Well, there you go.

Professor Peters: Why thank you.

Deshawn: Well, I have some more resting to do. Gotta keep my body temp on the level after what happened.

Professor Peters: Be safe.(Deshawn turns to walk away, but the Professor call him) Deshawn. (Deshawn turns to him) It's good to have you back.

Deshawn: (He looks to his side for a moment and gently chuckles) It's good to be back. (Deshawn walks up to his friends. Jose quickly grabs his arm. The moment he does, Deshawn tries to hold back wincing in pain. Erika quickly notices)

Jose: What the hell fool? I thought you had to rest for a few days? Do you want me to whup your ass?

Deshawn: I know I deserve the beat down. Then I thought, what better way to piss off the people that put me in the hospital, then proving that it takes a lot more than a few childish antics to get rid of me.

Jose: What you should be counting on is how it takes for you to get back in bed before I put you in a coma from beating the piss out of you.

Deshawn: Once again, thank you for yet another threat on my life.

Quinn: What are friends for fool? Why you still here anyway? You already shocked us. What other reason you got for sticking around?

Deshawn: Just a few. Stacey was one of them.

Jose: So, are you staying until the end of class? (From across the classroom Marcus looks at Deshawn)

Deshawn: (He rubs his chin and looks behind him to see Marcus staring at him. Marcus nods his head to him. Deshawn gently does the same and looks back to Jose) No, thanks to you, I have to finish that nice fat stack of homework I missed while being incapacitated in the hospital.

Quinn: So you're heading out?

Deshawn: (He gets up from his seat) Yeah. I got a few days left until I'm officially in welcome back status. I'll catch you all later. (He walks up the stairs and out of the classroom. Once the door closes, Deshawn closes his eyes and takes a deep breath. Seconds later he falls to the ground in pain. Kevin quickly grabs him and helps him up into a wheelchair)

Kevin: See, I told your ass this was a bad idea.

Deshawn: I had to.

Kevin: Just cause you wanna tell everybody that you ain't dead don't mean that you gotta do the same thing by coming here. Damn it boy, you haven't even fully thawed out yet.

Deshawn: I'll try to remember that next time.

Kevin: Your ass better. Let's get you back in bed man.

Deshawn: Works for me. (Kevin pushes Deshawn's wheelchair and proceeds to exit the school)

Kevin: Did you get the response you wanted?

Deshawn: More than I expected.

Kevin: Was it worth it?

Deshawn: (He scoffs) Every last second.

Kevin: Good. then let this be the last time this happens.

Deshawn: Amen to that. (Later on that night, he is sitting at his desk doing his homework. A few moments later and there is a knock at the door. Deshawn puts his pencil down and goes to open it) What's up man? (Jose walks in)

Jose: Not much bro, just checking up on you.

Deshawn: Why would you knock, don't you live here too?

Jose: Yeah well, I didn't want you to think that people were just barging in right after you got out of the hospital and what not.

Deshawn: Well, thanks for your consideration. (He walks back to his desk. Jose sits on his bed)

Jose: So, how have you been?

Deshawn: Good. I still get a little shaky at times from what happened, but luckily it's starting to wear off.

Jose: That's good. I know you might get a lot of this, but why would you do what you did?

Deshawn: I don't know. Once I opened the door to Stacey's room and saw what I saw, I guess my mind just snapped. All I could think about was me not wanting to hurt anyone, but only hurt myself. I'm not the type of person that just goes off on some kind of killing spree just because he's mad at himself. I suppose that my rage only forces the urge for me to want to die and no one else. That's how people who feel like I did do what they do. All my life I always knew that violence never solved anything. The bad part is, that the more I don't condone it, the more other people do everything they can to push me to.

Jose: Why won't you try to at least let people know what your limits are?

Deshawn: Because every time I did, it just gave people more of a reason to push me further down. Taking a stand never helped me. I could've just gave in and beat the hell out of both of them, but what would that do?

Jose: Prove one hell of a good point!

Deshawn: What point? There is none. Haven't you ever heard the saying that violence begets more violence?

Jose: So causing enough damage to nearly kill yourself again is the answer to that?

Deshawn: Yes! Don't you get it? Bad things always find their way to me! Every time I get a good feeling about things, it goes to hell. My family, Renee, Stacey! All of it! Remembering a time where I can actually struggle at trying to think of last time I felt depressed. Why is that so hard for me to have? I ask myself those questions everyday and I am tired of it. I'm sick of hiding all of this bullshit! I don't want it anymore.

Jose: So is that it? You wanted out? You wanted to end everything over a bitch? What kind of shit is this? This is not the D I knew of long ago. I remember a time where you just got out of a relationship and every time that we hung out everyone was on you. You had this new mind set on things. I remember you stopped caring about the bad things and did everything you could to make what ever time we had together as friends seem like we were brothers. Do you remember how many times you were willing to fight with more people than even I could take because they would talk down to you? Almost every time a fight would almost break out, you were the only one who would stand face to face with the biggest of the group and still show no fear. People who think so badly of themselves would never do what you do. I've seen people that were in the same position that you were in that have told me how much of an inspiration you are to them. I overheard a guy talking about the bad stuff that you would and do you know the most shocking thing that I heard him say was? I wonder how D does it? Do you have any idea what that means? It proves that anyone who was ever in your position can get out of it. No pills can do it, only you can and you have proved that fact every damn day.

Deshawn: I may have proved it, but stuff like that you just can't erase. I did change the way I saw things, but I can't change the way I am. I can tell the world that I don't care because I really don't. They did just fine without me. Every time I tried to get myself to belong I always got kicked right back out. So I figured why even try to. I walked my own path and found my own way, but in the long run, you're always stuck walking it alone.

Jose: So what now?

Deshawn: When I was in the hospital, I realized that no matter what happens, I will always have that emotional scar that will haunt me for the rest of my life and I can't change that. The only thing I can do is keep on living, and worrying about only the bad things will only cloud the important things I want in my life.

Jose: So what exactly do you want?

Deshawn: I haven't made it that far yet.

Jose: Fair enough. Are we still planning on the prom deal?

Deshawn: I told you before; we're not doing the limo thing.

Jose: So the taxi is better?

Deshawn: (He laughs) No. We can do the limo thing, but can we at least make it sound a little more realistic?

Jose: Fine with me, as long as you're going.

Deshawn: Which I am.

Jose: Good. I'll leave you to your books. I got some stuff to do.

Deshawn: All right.

Jose: You're still going right?

Deshawn: Of course.

Jose: You better. (He gets up and walks to the door) I want you to remember something, bitches come and go, but friends are forever.

Deshawn: (He laughs) You're learning well young Jedi.

Jose: Hey, I learned from the best. You're still going right?

Deshawn: I said yeah.

Jose: Just making sure. I'll see you.

Deshawn: All right later.

Jose: Peace out. (He closes the door. Deshawn goes back to working on his homework. Moments later the door opens)

Deshawn: Damn it man, I already told you that (He turns around in his chair, but he stops before he can finish his sentence as he sees who it is at the door. It's Stacey) oh. (He turns back around) If you're looking for the train, the rest of the jocks live down the hall.

Stacey: I deserve that. Can I at least talk to you for a second please?

Deshawn: You deserve a lot of things. Good thing my time for you is already expired. Speaking of which, your second is up. Now get the fuck out of my room.

Stacey: D, I'm so sorry. I need to tell you how bad I feel about all of this. I never meant for any of this to happen.

Deshawn: So, you never meant to get naked and ravished by another guy knowing full that you were with me? (Stacey tries to answer, but Deshawn cuts her off) Let me take a guess on what your answer might be here. He talked to you, made you feel special, promised you a lot of things and you could do nothing, but eat it. He starts to tell you some stupid shit like how if you were with him, everything would be so much better. Then, after you seal the deal, he turns Casper and vanishes and all of those promises are gone. Then all that's left is nothing. All due to the fact that you willingly wanted to destroy a relationship that you wanted me to think that we had by becoming a full-fledged whore. Is that about close to it?

Stacey: It is, but there was more.

Deshawn: Wonderful. I take it that he handled your speed better than me. (She is silent) I guess that answers it.

Stacey: You're right. I never meant to do it on purpose.

Deshawn: Really? So then, ditching me at the party to go get a piece of ass by some other guy was never on purpose. The funniest thing is; that it was from the same guy who put me in the hospital in the first place. That wasn't on purpose? Why, I never would've guessed.

Stacey: I didn't know.

Deshawn: What's there to know? You did it anyway. All of this couldn't have been planned before you met me.

Stacey: It wasn't.

Deshawn: That's right, I forgot. It all happened so fast right? (He gets up and walks to her) A piece of information for you; a person like you may have waited a few days, weeks, or even a few months to find someone like me. I have waited years. Now that I felt like the waiting is over, I get put back at the end of the line again and I hate that. Now, I just don't care. (He takes a step closer) I especially don't care about you anymore. I don't care to the point where I would rather die this very second, then to have to see your face at the end of the day. You want me to trust you again, better luck with some other sucker because you lost mine for a long time.

Stacey: What can I do to get that back?

Deshawn: For right now, you can get out. Until I think you're worth my time again and that might not be for a long time.

Stacey: I can understand that. What ever it is that I have to do to be your friend again I want to do it. I want you to know how sorry I really am. I want you to trust me again.

Deshawn: Trust is a fragile word like I once was. Trust is something that you have to prove yourself worthy of and you broke that. I can try to trust you again, but never like I used to.

Stacey: What do I have to do to get that back?

Deshawn: As of right now, nothing. There's no way I could trust you the way I did after what you put me through. You forced me back into a hole I promised myself I would never go back into. That I can not accept. What you did to me brought things I spent my life to forget. The things you made me remember forced me to relive the one thing I didn't want anymore, and that was for me to die. To ask someone to forgive something that big, you can't just wash away. To think, after everything that we went through, I was ready to give you everything you could ever want from a man. I was ready to give up the hate that I had inside for people just to be with you. Yet, you threw it all away over a joke. I hope that makes you feel better about yourself. Now if you'll excuse me, I have some homework to finish. (He turns around and walks back to his desk. He sits down) If there isn't anything else you want to tell me, (He points behind him) the door's over there. (Stacey sheds a tear)

Stacey: Can you look at me and tell me that at least a small part of you can forgive me?

Deshawn: I could, but if I did I wouldn't be able to tell which one of your faces I would be talking to.

Stacey: All right. So, I guess this really is it. Before I go, I need to tell you something, I didn't lie about how I felt about you. Everything I said came from my heart. Marcus may have used my body, but he never took my heart the way you did. I wish I could take it back, but I can't. I want to so badly that it hurts. I had to use every once of strength I had inside to come here to tell you how sorry I am. D, I (Deshawn cuts her off before she can finish)

Deshawn: Don't even say it! Don't you even think about saying that word to me! It took me all that I had to use that word too, but what makes it so different, is that never wasted it like you did. When I finally found the strength to say it, a piece if my soul went with it because I thought it was worth using it this time. Now that I know that it wasn't, I'm done with it, but most importantly, I'm definitely done with you. So you can go now. (A moment of silence between the two) Why are you still here? Please do not tell me that you're using this awkward silence to shed tears, hoping to gain what little sympathy that I have left. (Stacey looks down for a moment and walks out of the room. She quickly jumps back because Erika stands on the opposite side of the hallway staring at her)

Erika: At last we meet again. You have no idea the things that I want to do to you. From the looks of it, what D did to you was far much worse that what I would've done. I would give you the whole, don't ever hurt him again routine, but I've got a feeling that you know that if you ever tried to, you would know that you won't be dealing him, you would be dealing with me. That is something that you really don't want.

Stacey: I know.

Erika: No, you don't. Right now, I'm trying to use every inch of kindness and decency to hold back the urge to beat the hell out of you. So please don't ruin it for me. Just remember whatever he said and go. (Stacey looks to Erika for a moment and walks away. Erika lets out a sigh and opens the door a crack. Deshawn stops and clenches a fist) It's me. Calm down.

Deshawn: I'm sorry. I'm just a little edgy right now after having her here.

Erika: I know. (She walks over to his bed and scoots next to him) Are you going to be all right?

Deshawn: It might take a little more time that I hoped for, but I think I can manage.

Erika: Here, (She pats next to her on the bed) come here and talk to me. (Deshawn gets up and takes of his shirt. He sits down for a moment and throws his shirt on the ground) What's wrong?

Deshawn: I wish I knew. After what happened, I can't think about anything the way I used to anymore. I just wish that I can just forget all of this.

Erika: I want to ask you something, why would you do what you did? Why would you want to leave us? I guess the most important question is, why would you want to leave me?

Deshawn: (He pauses for a moment) Do you know what it means to feel alone? I'm not talking about a time where no one was around or no one would talk to you. I mean the emptiness that a person feels inside. The feeling that there is nothing that makes the person who they are. Makes them feel like they don't have a soul to call their own. It's like a scar that won't heal and it's always there to make you remember that no matter how hard you try, you can never forget. I spend the last few years praying for the day that it would finally go away, but it never does. All I wanted in my life is to feel wanted. To feel like I belong, but every time I do, I'm always forced to start over from the beginning, never being able to see the end. Once I walked to her room that day, I knew that there was something telling me not to open the door. I was searching for every reason I had to stop and turn back around thinking that if I pretended to be happy I wouldn't be so afraid anymore. Once I walked inside and saw what was happening, I became that child again. I (He stops as he tries to stop himself from crying) relived every single moment that I thought that I no longer remembered. I can't do this anymore. (He stands up and leans against the wall by the door. Erika watches him as her eyes grow watery as well) All my life, I've always felt incomplete. The times I share with you and the guys are the best times I've ever had, but in the end, I can't shake the feeling that I would be living to witness what I can't have. When I first met St … (He stops himself from saying her name as his voice begins to crack) her, I thought that I finally found that. (He clenches his fist tightly) Then when that bitch (He slams his fist against the wall, but Erika is focus is placed only on what Deshawn is saying. She watches him as he speaks and notices how hard he is trying not to cry) did what she did, I just lost it. I don't want this pain anymore. I don't want these feelings. I just don't want to be alone anymore. (He breaks down and cries as he slides to the ground covering his face as he sobs. Erika gets up from the bed and walks to him. She kneels down and slowly pulls his arms away to get him to look at her)

Erika: There is something that I need to tell you. It's the promise that I said that I couldn't tell you. On the day where you promised me that you would give yourself anymore reminders, I promised that I wouldn't do the one thing that I couldn't stop fighting with myself. I promised that I would never fall in love with you. Over the past few days I've learned something as well, you have always been the man that I ever wanted in my life. (She gently rubs a side his face) I tried to hide it for so long, but I don't want to anymore because I love you. (She kisses him. They embrace for a moment and Deshawn slowly moves back)

Deshawn: Thank you.

Erika: For what?

Deshawn: For being my reason. I don't know what I would've done without you.

Erika: I should be thanking you.

Deshawn: For what?

Erika: For being your reason. You mean so much to me. You do have a reason, you always did. You're smart, funny, charming when you want to. That and you know how to make people feel special about who they are. Not that many people around that can do the things that you do. You never lived by the rules. You made your own. That's what makes you so different, so fearless. You were never afraid to be yourself. That's what this place needed to see. A true independent. You may have lost a lot of things, but you have gained so much. Never tell yourself different.

Deshawn: I'm so sorry.

Erika: You don't have to apologize for anything.

Deshawn: I have to. When Renee was taken from me, I never thought that I could happy again, until the day when we first became close. I wanted to tell you how much I cared for you, but something inside told me not to. In the end, I guess that was a good thing because I wouldn't be scared to tell you that I love you too.

Erika: D. (She hugs him as Deshawn continues to sob. She sits down next to him while continuing to hold him) Just promise me one thing.

Deshawn: What?

Erika: Promise me that you will get Becky back for this.

Deshawn: (He laughs) I put those wheels in motion once I got out of class today.

Erika: What did you do?

Deshawn: A master never reveals his secrets. You'll find out soon or later.

CHAPTER 20

▼

Deshawn Narrarates: What's one of the important nights before graduation? That's right prom night. Good times. The last time I remember wearing a suit was class picture day in grade school. The bad part about it was that the other kids kept mistaking me for Steve Urkel. Hell, I even had the high-waters pants to match. The best part about tonight, is that the most gorgeous woman on her way here to be with me tonight. The only downside is me wondering how long does it take a woman to put a dress on.

(Months pass. Students of the college walk inside a large building. The women wear dresses and the men in freshly pressed suits. Inside, Deshawn walks down a set of stairs and to Jose and Quinn as they stand at the bottom of them)

Jose: I thought that all of were coming here together?

Deshawn: I know. Erika was so hell bent on coming here on her own, that I just said forget it.

Jose: I thought you two were dating now?

Deshawn: We are, but hey, I never argue with a woman.

Quinn: Did you call her?

Deshawn: No, I just figured that I'll wait. (Jose looks at the top of the stairs as Deshawn speaks) I trying to work on this whole rebound dating thing, which is going very well, don't get me wrong. (Quinn looks up as well) Believe me, I really do care a lot for Erika and I happy that we're together now. (Jose cuts him off before he can finish)

Jose: Could you shut up please?

Deshawn: What? Why? (Jose does nothing, but point behind Deshawn. Deshawn turns around and looks to the top of the stairs. Erika slowly walks down the steps wearing a very elegant dress and her hair flows beautifully to her shoulders. She walks up to the three as they all look in awe) Hi.

Erika: Hi guys. (Jose and Quinn wave to her. She walks up and kisses the two of them on the cheek then grabs Deshawn by the ears and passionately kisses him) Sorry I got here so late. Getting this dress on was a pain in my heavily stair-mastered ass. (She points to Quinn and Jose) And if the next words out of your mouths aren't compliments, I'm implanting these heels dead in your cornholes got it?

Jose: We got it. Damn, you don't have to be hostile all of the time.

Erika: I have to maintain my position here. Just because me and D are the hottest ones here doesn't mean people should be getting the wrong idea.

Quinn: Which is what?

Erika: That anyone here can mess with us. So where's you're women at?

Jose: Getting us drinks.

Erika: That's nice. You keep telling yourself that. (She looks to Deshawn and smiles) Does it look all right? (She turns around to show the whole thing and the group is still speechless) I'll take that as a yes. D, (She holds out her hand) shall we?

Deshawn: We shall. (He holds her hand and guides her to the dance floor)

Jose: Damn.

Erika: (She turns her head to Jose and Quinn and she walks away) You boys be good until we get back, okay? (Deshawn and Erika find a spot for them and begin to dance slowly)

Deshawn: I must say that you really do look amazing.

Erika: Thank you. So do you. Now, would you please tell me this payback plan of yours that you have ingeniously hid from me?

Deshawn: If you must know, I ran into Marcus.

Erika: Marcus? The one who's ass I kicked? But didn't he … (Deshawn cuts her off)

Deshawn: Yeah, that one. Anyway, he apologized to me and told me what happened, letting me know that Becky used him and that he didn't like her all that much anymore. He told me some things and I told him some things, then we came to the conclusion to do the only option that we came to.

Erika: And that was?

Deshawn: Let's just say that word gets around quick when you find out that the girl that you call your friend enjoys using the wrong people.

Erika: I guess the most important question is; why was Mark so pissed at you anyway?

Deshawn: Apparently, she told him that I said that she's got diseases worse than the monkey in "Outbreak". Which is probably true anyway, but when someone spreads a false rumor where the risk of losing your dick is involved would pretty much piss anyone off. Once I found that out, I did what any smart man would do. I just told the truth, meaning all of it.

Erika: You didn't!

Deshawn: I did. These lips reveal all when it comes to further harm on my body. Besides, you know my motto on payback.

Erika: How does it go again? If you push me, I push back ten times harder.

Deshawn: Unfortunately for Becky, she decided kick me while I was down. So I had to add a side of over the limit vengeance too.

Erika: Will you tell me already? The suspense is killing me.

Deshawn: All right, since Marcus knew the truth about Becky, all there was left to do was tell it to everyone else. He already knows she's loose.

Erika: Doesn't everyone already know that?

Deshawn: Right, but what Becky never knew was that the people she was messing with were also messing with her friends too.

Erika: You didn't!

Deshawn: I did.

Erika: Then that means ...

Deshawn: Exactly. Either she goes into quarantine or her little rat squad would have something special in common after all.

Erika: You are so evil.

Deshawn: You know you like it.

Erika: Maybe so, but there is one extra thing that I like even more.

Deshawn: What's that?

Erika: Being in love with you.

Deshawn: You know, for the first time in my life, I think that I can finally say something that I never though I could ever say without being afraid to.

Erika: What's that?

Deshawn: I love you.

Erika: I love you too. (They kiss as the music plays and everyone dances around them. Days pass and Deshawn sits outside on a park bench with a small box next him. He is talking to someone on his phone as he goes through a stack of papers)

CHAPTER 21

▼

Deshawn Narrarates: Graduation. One of the best days to have. So much craziness to occur in so little time here. I feel good about it though. I feel less weighed down now. I feel stronger, more at peace. I guess a better way to describe it, is that I feel more myself and how I'm supposed to be. The only thing to do now is give the woman that means so much to me, something that she deserves. I took the job from my professor still. He's got me teaching the new students the importance of thinking on your own. It's funny because at first I thought that no one would listen, but remembering what happened on the last day of class changed everything.

Deshawn: Yeah I know right? I'm proud of myself too. So, how's everyone else been? Really now? That's cool. No problem. Thanks. Take care dad. Bye. (He stops at one of his papers. On the front page, it has in red ink an A plus and a notation from his professor which reads

Professor Peters: Congratulations Deshawn. You have been the only student to speak about the things that no one could ever talk about. Your lack of restrictions on the truth has opened the eyes of so many people and you deserve to be called truly, the most intellectual person this school has ever had. Your independence and free will has generated a whole new way of life to learn to understand. I have a good feeling that the new soul that you have placed in my classroom will give you the courage to spread it across the world. Good luck with your plans for the future. One more thing; I expect to see you in my class next year to help teach the new students. Great minds are hard to find.

Deshawn: (He reads to himself the paper he wrote) What defines me. Everything does. I live my life by every road. Giving myself the opportunity to be a part of everything that life has to offer. What makes me who I am isn't the clothes I wear or what I watch or listen to. It's how well I evolve with the life that I am living. Over the years, I have learned a lot of things. I've learned that no matter the circumstance, everyone can feel pain. It isn't because you dress differently than other people or because you live life outside of what people call normal. Everyone no matter where they come from can suffer from a pain so terrible that they would rather take their own life than keep living it. I have been a victim of living in a world where being who you want to be makes you an outcast. By taking that and harnessing that energy has made me into who I am today. I am a man who refuses to live in a world where being different makes you the words of negativity. I am an individual which from what I've seen, the world knows almost nothing about. (He sees Stacey sitting at her desk hidden, but still paying attention to what he says) I am who I am and nothing can change that. I am me. (He sees Marcus sitting in the back of the classroom sitting next to Becky) I stand on the throne that I made on my own and not on one built by others. There is no group, no click, no sets, no affiliations, no congregations and definitely no followers I run with. (He subtly winks to Marcus as he looks back down at his papers. Marcus leans over to one of his friends and whispers in his ear. The other student looks in shock as he looks to Becky. Once Marcus leans back in his seat, the other student leans over to some more of his friends and whispers to them as well. One by one, more and more students whisper to each other from all around Becky and her friends. Becky looks in confusion as she tries to find out what's going on. She leans up to someone in front of her trying to see what's going on, but the person ignores her. She doesn't notice that one of the other students has just finished whispering something to one of her friends as she sits back in her chair. Becky looks to her friend still confused as few people give her glances of disgust. Her friend shakes her head and stands up to move to a different seat in the classroom. Becky looks to Marcus)

Becky: Marcus, what the hell is going on? Why are people looking at me this way?

Marcus: Don't ask me. (He points to Deshawn) Ask him. Since none of your friends can trust you anymore, why not trying trusting your supposed enemy?

Deshawn: I lead the pack and only I can set the pace. Everyone else who runs with me never follow, but only run as leaders of their own. I appreciate the gratitude that I have been given by being told that I was an inspiration to people. By giving people the strength to keep going during times where they couldn't. By expressing my way of life in ways no one has seen before, things like this make me who I am. Being I am my own man and that's all that matters. (Deshawn lets out a chuckle as he rolls up the papers and places them in his side pocket. Erika walks up from behind him and jumps on the bench to sit down next to him. She gives him a hug)

Erika: Happy graduation baby.

Deshawn: Happy graduation.

Erika: What's wrong?

Deshawn: Nothing. I was just thinking about some thing running through my head.

Erika: Like what?

Deshawn: How things came to be over the past few months. So much has happened in so little time, that it makes me think about what everyone has been telling me. The pain that I suffered finally made me realize that I really am an inspiration to people. I've never really been told that before. It makes me feel that I actually do have a place in the world you know. Like I finally do have a reason. I kind of scares me.

Erika: Why does it scare you?

Deshawn: Because for the first time in my life, I'm happy. All the pain, all the fear, all the doubt is gone. It feels like it never happened and it feels so awkward for me. I came from being a scared child, to a one man army against stupidity. That and oddly enough, being told that I can uplift people who feel the lowest just as I once did.

Erika: I'm proud of you.

Deshawn: I'm proud of myself too. (Erika sees the small box sitting next to him)

Erika: What's that?

Deshawn: (He looks to the box and picks it up. He looks at it as he talks to her) This? This is something that I wanted to give you for a while now. Here. (She takes it)

Erika: What is it?

Deshawn: Let's just say that I paid a lot of attention to the things that you have been telling me.

Erika: What are you saying?

Deshawn: You'll find out in the note I put on it. I'm going to go find the guys. (He gets up from the bench, kisses her on the cheek and walks away. Erika pulls off the piece of paper and unfolds it. She reads it aloud)

Erika: Two things that I want you to know. First; I want you to know that I love you more than anything in this world. Never forget that. You have giving me the feelings that I thought I lost so long ago and I thank you for that. Second; on the day where I went to the roof, did anyone check to see which one of the rings I chose? (She stops reading) What? (She slowly unwraps the paper showing a ring box. She slowly opens it. Her eyes widen in shock to see that the ring Deshawn didn't choose was the one Erika liked the most. Her eyes begin to get watery as she covers her mouth as she is speechless. She quickly gets off of the bench and runs to Deshawn) D! (Deshawn turns around. Erika rushes into his arms and they embrace as Erika continues to cry)

Deshawn: I guess you understand how I feel about you now.

Erika: Less talking, more kissing.

Deshawn: I love you too. (She kisses him. Moments later, Jose and Quinn walk up from behind the two)

Jose: Damn it man! Quit with the make-out session already. You two have been on each other ever since you've been going out.

Erika: (She lets go of him and holds his hand) Hush up peasant boy! Don't be jealous.

Quinn: He'll try to hide it next time.

Deshawn: I was just about to look for you two.

Jose: So, were we. (He pulls out a camera from his pocket) Graduation pictures.

Deshawn: Sweet!

Jose: All right then, let's do this. (He runs to the bench and places the camera on it. He sets the timer and the group stands together) So what should we dedicate this to?

Quinn: To a new future.

Erika: To a new life.

Deshawn: To a new beginning and I know just how to start it. You guys ready?

Quinn: Let's do it. (Seconds before the camera flashes to take the picture, the group all raise up their middle finger to it. After the picture is taken, Erika claps and grabs Deshawn's hand)

Erika: Well, that was fun. Let's go D.

Jose: (He walks to the camera not looking at the two) Leave now and I kick your teeth in. Erika, since you were the first one who wanted to leave, you're the first one working the camera. Now take it and deal with it.

Erika: (She takes the camera from him as she laughs) You are so lucky that we're best friends.

Jose: Cause if we weren't, I would be your pimp instead of D. All right, we got more to use, so let's get this show on the road! (More pictures are taken of the group all doing different poses and playing around. Either as a group, or by themselves, all takes their own unique style pose as the pictures are taken. Erika and Deshawn take their picture together as a happy couple by either hugging, kissing, or playing around as well. Moments later, Jose runs back to the camera to set it again) All right guys, last one. (He runs back the group) This one should be special.

Quinn: The topper of our lives.

Erika: So what should this one be dedicated to?

Quinn: Happy graduation.

Jose: Friends forever.

Erika: To the love of my life.

Deshawn: I got it. This one (He looks to his friends) is to family. (He looks to the camera as they all stand arm and arm. He winks and releases a small grin and the final picture is taken of all of them together)

978-0-595-44957-●
0-595-44957-3

Made in the USA
Las Vegas, NV
27 March 2022

46379087R00111